Sean's Redemption

Dark Patriots 3.5 (Novella)

Ciara St James

Copyright

Printed in the United States of America
Editing by Mary Kern @ Ms. K Edits
Book cover by Kiwi Kreations

Blurb

Sean and Cassidy's ultimate love story has only been hinted at but never told in their friends and family's books. Take a trip down memory lane and discover what made Sean finally declare his true feelings for Cassidy. Did her time with the Warriors MC in Dublin Falls and a certain biker named Falcon do it? Or was it the dangerous mission she helped with? Or were Sean's eyes open long before those two things happened? Find out Sean's true reason for not declaring himself long ago.

See what Cassidy was forced to do in order to find happiness for herself and what her choices caused Sean to do. Theirs has been a love story years in the making. Join them as they welcome their second child into the world and take a stroll down memory lane, recalling what got them there and the bumps and tears along the way. You asked for it, and now here it is, Sean and Cassidy of the Dark Patriots' story. Come read Sean's Redemption.

Warning

This book is intended for adult readers. It explores some topics may not be to everyone's taste. Subjects considered taboo by some will be explored. It contains foul language and adult situations and may even include things such as stalking, assault, torture, kidnapping, and murder, which may trigger some readers. Sexual situations are graphic. If these themes aren't what you like to read or you find them upsetting, this book isn't for you. There is no cheating or cliffhangers, and it has a HEA.

Dedication

This is for the readers who asked me more than once, will Sean and Cassidy ever get a book to tell us how they got together? I kept saying no, but then this popped into my head. I guess this teaches me not to say never. I hope you enjoy this look back.

Dark Patriots Members/ Ladies:

Mark O'Rourke (Undertaker) w/ Sloan
Sean Walterson w/ Cassidy
Gabe Pagett w/ Gemma
Griffin Voss w/ Hadley
Benedict Madris w/ TBD
Heath Rugger w/ TBD
Justin Becker w/ TBD
Beau Powers w/ TBD

Reading Order

For Dublin Falls Archangel's Warriors MC (DFAW), Hunters Creek Archangel's Warriors MC (HCAW), Iron Punishers MC (IPMC), Dark Patriots (DP), Pagan Souls of Cherokee MC (PSCMC), & Horsemen of Wrath MC (HOW)

Terror's Temptress DFAW 1
Savage's Princess DFAW 2
Steel & Hammer's Hellcat DFAW 3
Menace's Siren DFAW 4
Ranger's Enchantress DFAW 5
Ghost's Beauty DFAW 6
Viper's Vixen DFAW 7
Devil Dog's Precious DFAW 8
Blaze's Spitfire DFAW 9
Smoke's Tigress DFAW 10
Hawk's Huntress DFAW 11
Bull's Duchess HCAW 1
Storm's Flame DFAW 12
Rebel's Firecracker HCAW 2
Ajax's Nymph HCAW 3
Razor's Wildcat DFAW 13
Capone's Wild Thing DFAW 14
Falcon's She-Devil DFAW 15
Demon's Hellion HCAW 4
Torch's Tornado DFAW 16
Voodoo's Sorceress DFAW 17

Reaper's Banshee IPMC 1
Bear's Beloved HCAW 5
Outlaw's Jewel HVAW 6
Undertaker's Resurrection DP 1
Agony's Medicine Woman PSCMC 1
Ink's Whirlwind IP 2
Payne's Goddess HCAW 7
Maverick's Kitten HCAW 8
Tiger & Thorn's Tempest DFAW 18
Dare's Doll PSC 2
Maniac's Imp IP 3
Tank's Treasure HCAW 9
Blade's Boo DFAW 19
Law's Valkyrie DFAW 20
Gabriel's Retaliation DP 2
Knight's Bright Eyes PSC 3
Joker's Queen HCAW 10
Bandit & Coyote's Passion DFAW 21
Sniper's Dynamo & Gunner's Diamond DFAW 22
Slash's Dove HCAW 11
Lash's Hurricane IP 4
Spawn's She-Wolf IP 5
Griffin's Revelation DP 3
Twisted's Storm PSC 4
Diablo's Vengeance HOW 1
Player's Juno HCAW 12
Sean's Redemption DP 3.5 (Novella)

For Ares Infidels MC

Sin's Enticement AIMC 1
Executioner's Enthrallment AIMC 2
Pitbull's Enslavement AIMC 3
Omen's Entrapment AIMC 4

Cuffs' Enchainment AIMC 5
Rampage's Enchantment AIMC 6
Wrecker's Ensnarement AIMC 7
Trident's Enjoyment AIMC 8
Fang's Enlightenment AIMC 9
Talon's Enamorment AIMC 10
Ares Infidels in NY AIMC 11
Phantom's Emblazonment AIMC 12
Saint's Enrapturement AIMC 13
Phalanx & Bullet's Entwinement AIMC 14
Torpedo's Entrancement AIMC 15
Boomer's Embroilment AIMC 16
Daredevil's Engulfment AIMC 17
Vicious, Ashes & Dragon's Entrenchment AIMC 18
Ruin's Embattlement AIMC 19 (end)

For O'Sheerans Mafia

Darragh's Dilemma
Cian's Complication
Aidan's Ardor
Aisling's Craving
Tiernan's Striving

House of Lustz

Mikhail's Playhouse
Hoss's Limits

Please follow Ciara on Facebook. For information on new releases & to catch up with Ciara, go to www.ciara-st-james.com or www.facebook.com/ciara.stjames.1 or https://www.facebook.com/groups/342893626927134 (Ciara St James Angels) or https://www.facebook.com/groups/923322252903958 (House of Lustz by Ciara St

James)   or   https://www.facebook.com/ groups/1404894160210851 (O'Sheeran Mafia by Ciara St James)

Cassidy: Chapter 1 - Present

I grimaced as I opened my eyes. The room was dark. I had no idea what time it was, but I knew it was still the middle of the night. Glancing to the right, I saw the red digital numbers on my alarm clock. It was two in the morning. As things became less foggy in my sleepy brain, I realized why I woke up. I had to pee. And not just pee, but piss like a racehorse, as the saying goes. I eased back the covers and wiggled to get myself to the edge of the mattress so that I could get up. It wasn't easy to do these days.

My feet never reached the ground before Sean popped out of bed. He rounded the corner of the bed and came to stand before me. "Cass, why didn't you wake me? Here, let me help you. I'm turning on your light," he warned seconds before my bedside lamp snapped on. The room was flooded with a yellow glow, which allowed me to see him clearly.

Even with my urinary urgency screaming at me, I wasn't able to help myself. I took several precious moments to run my eyes over him. It never failed. No matter what or how long we'd been together, he always aroused me. I gave him my hands.

"I can go to the bathroom alone, Sean. I'm not crippled. I'm just pregnant with your second spawn, who loves to lay on and kick his momma's bladder," I informed him sarcastically.

He merely chuckled, gripped my hands, and boosted me to my feet. I would never admit it to him, but I adored how he treated me—well, at least I did most of the time. Whenever I was pregnant, he became even more protective, and I had to make threats to keep him from smothering me. He held my hands firmly with one of his and wrapped the other around my back.

"I know you're not crippled, but you're not as steady as you usually are, either, babe. The baby is throwing you off balance. The last thing I want is for you to fall and hurt yourself or the baby. We're in the home stretch. Just a week to go," he reminded me as if I needed one.

"Yeah, we are, and I can't wait. Ooh, hurry before I piss myself," I hissed as I tried to waddle faster. In the end, I barely lowered myself to the toilet seat before I was peeing. Did he leave me alone to handle my business? No. He stood there with his arms crossed, waiting for me to be done.

"Can't a woman get some privacy?" I complained, knowing the answer.

"Nope. I know everything about you. There's nothing for you to be embarrassed about. I've touched, kissed, licked, and fucked every square inch of your beautiful body, Cassidy."

His words were enough to turn me on. God, why did he have to do that? We weren't supposed to be having sex since we were so close to my due date, but God, did I want to. "Stop saying stuff like that! You're making me horny, and we can't do anything about it," I reminded him as I maneuvered to wipe myself. He moved toward me, but my scowl froze him in place.

"I can wipe myself. Don't think for a second that

I'm going to let you do it. Yeesh, is there no indignity we women don't have to endure?" I muttered as I wiped, then stood.

I'd given up on wearing underwear at six months. All they did was cut into me or get in the way. Sean loved it. He hated I wore anything, but with Noah, we couldn't sleep naked like we used to. I dropped my nightie and then moved over to the sink. I allowed him to turn on the water for me.

His arms came around my middle from behind. He kissed the back of my neck. I shivered at the sensations that tiny kiss sent blazing throughout my body. "Cassidy, there's nothing I wouldn't do for you. Taking care of you and our children is my top priority. Come back to bed. You need your sleep, Foxy."

His nickname for me always made me smile. I was turning to face him when a pain shot through my stomach from my back to my belly button. I gasped and hunched forward.

"Cass, what's wrong?" he asked in a panic.

Before I could tell him, I felt warm liquid running down my legs. Oh shit, I guess there would be no going back to bed to sleep tonight. I gripped one of his hands and squeezed.

"It looks like we're having a baby. My water just broke. We need to get me dressed and put our things in the car, then head to the hospital in a bit. I'll call Dr. Maggio's answering service so they can let him know. My overnight bag is in the hallway closet by the door. Why don't you get it while I clean up and get some clothes on?"

I saw his incredulous expression in the mirror we happened to be facing. "There's no fucking way I'm leaving you alone to do shit! I'm sending out the bat signal, calling the doctor's service, and then I'll help you get cleaned up and dressed," he half-growled.

I rolled my eyes. What he called the bat signal was a text group he created forever ago. It included me, him, my brother, Undertaker, and his wife, Sloan. They weren't the only ones. His other two best friends, Gabe and Griffin, along with their wives, Gemma and Hadley, were part of it, too. I joked around all the time about where the signal in the sky was. Guess what his favorite cartoon was as a kid?

"I want you to sit back down until I get back with my phone," he ordered.

I didn't fight him. I knew it was no use. He flipped down the toilet lid after he moved me back to it. He lowered me down and then rushed out of the room. I wanted to giggle but knew he wouldn't find this situation funny.

As I waited, I rubbed my stomach. "Not much longer, little guy. I can't wait to meet you in person, and I know your daddy can't. Noah asks every day if today is the day he gets his baby brother. Wait until we tell him yes."

Speaking of Noah, I hoped we wouldn't wake him up. He was down the hall sleeping. Our almost-three-year-old usually slept like the dead, but with our luck, tonight he wouldn't. My thoughts were cut off by Sean bursting back into the bathroom. He was texting like mad one-handed. Lord, I couldn't do that to save my soul, but he and the others seemed to have taken a class on how to do it.

"How're you doing?" he asked.

"I'm fine. Just want to get this mess off me and the floor."

"Let me and the others worry about the mess. Come on, they'll be here soon. Do I need to call an ambulance?"

"No ambulance. I'm not about to pop him out any second, Sean. We have time."

"Okay, but if anything changes, tell me. Getting you in the shower is the easiest way to get you clean. Let me start the water." He moved to turn it on.

As it got hot, he stripped off my nightie and his underwear. Jesus, the sight of his cock made me ache in a whole different way. I wasn't able to stop myself from grasping him. I stroked up and down his length a couple of times. He groaned and instantly hardened.

"Baby, stop. We don't have time for this, although it kills me to say that. We need to get you clean and ready to go. Do you know what Mark would do if he came in here to find me fucking his sister while she's in labor? Undertaker would come out, and I'd be dead. I'm still not sure he likes the fact I stole his little sister and dirty her up on a regular day, let alone when you're pregnant."

I laughed. "Mark knows you didn't take advantage of me, Sean. I was the one who did the chasing, remember?"

"I do, but it wasn't all you. Not in the end," he reminded me.

He got me into the shower before I could go down memory lane. He swiftly, although gently, washed me. By the time I was clean and dried and we were both dressed, his phone buzzed. He glanced at it.

"Your brother is here," he said as he replied with his text.

I never heard their footsteps. One moment, we were alone in the bedroom, and the next, Mark and Sloan were there. She hurried over to hug me. Mark was holding their barely awake son, Caleb, in his arms. He was a year younger than Noah. Caleb gave me a sleepy smile and then closed his eyes.

"Is she ready to go? Where's the ambulance?" Mark barked like a drill instructor.

"I don't need an ambulance. We have plenty of time. Now that you're here, we can get sorted to go. Sloan, are you still alright with staying here and watching Noah for us?"

"I sure am. Of course, I'd love to be there to see every second of this one's journey into the world, but I can wait. At least Mark will be there. Honey, why don't you slip Caleb into bed with Noah? They need their sleep. While you do that, I'll help Cassidy. Sean, why don't you get her go-bag from down in the closet?"

Both men were less than happy, but they did as she asked. I knew if they didn't, Sloan's inner badass would've come out and made them. My sister-in-law was no pushover. As they left, I sighed in relief.

"Have I told you lately that you're my favorite sister-in-law?"

She laughed. "No, but technically, I'm your only one, so I take it as a given. Gemma and Hadley don't count. They don't have to put up with your brother. You should give me a medal," she teased.

That made me laugh. I sat down on the bed. Sloan puttered around getting last-minute things together as I called them out to her. She'd reduced my stress by merely being here. It was a matter of minutes before I had the other four arriving in our bedroom. Gabe and Gemma had a sleeping four-month-old Greer with them. She was so cute and had her daddy wrapped around her finger as tightly as her momma had him.

Griffin and a pregnant Hadley rounded them out. They had about six months to go before we got our hands on their first baby. I was hoping for another girl to help Greer corral our sons. The men thought it was the opposite, that the boys would look after the girls. We let them believe that, but we knew the truth.

Hadley, Gemma, and Sloan had worked out the babysitting details weeks ago. Sloan would take the first round. Later, she'd traded off with Hadley and, finally, Gemma. Eventually, the dads would watch the kids, but they all saw themselves as my brothers, and there was no way they'd remain at the house while I had my son. The ladies understood and were great about it.

After hugging and kissing the new arrivals, I knew it was time to get on the road. It wasn't due to the baby coming, but my man seemed about to lose it. He was pacing. "Let's get this mission done," I quipped.

Like magic, I was swept up and away. I was hustled outside and into our car. I had to threaten Sean to keep him from carrying me to it. Mark joined us. Gabe, Gemma, Hadley, and Griff got into Gabe's vehicle. On the way to the hospital, I had to keep reminding my man not to speed that we had plenty of time. Whenever I did, he'd barely ease off the accelerator.

I felt for the poor staff when we arrived. We came through the doors into the maternity ward, which was where I'd been told to go when I went into labor, like a military platoon. Dr. Maggio had answered Sean's text on the way here and reiterated where I was to go. Four massive, dangerous men come storming in, and you'd want to hide. I knew the staff wanted to. I wasn't sure why all the staff was that way. Several had been here when I had Noah and Greer and Caleb were born. They, at least, should be used to the Dark Patriots. Looking at my entourage's faces, you'd think they were storming an enemy's citadel. Their scowls were somewhat off-putting, so maybe I shouldn't expect the staff to be at ease.

"Psst, smile. You're gonna make the staff freak and run. Then what will we do?" I hissed at them.

"I'll drag their fucking asses back," Sean muttered before facing a nurse who was standing at the nurses' station.

All the others were crowded behind it. She was standing tall. I was rather shocked. She didn't appear to be the oldest, maybe a couple of years younger than my thirty. Many of those behind her were older. She exuded authority.

"Where the hell is Dr. Maggio?" Sean snapped at her.

"Sir, keep your voice down. This is a hospital, not a bar. Dr. Maggio is on his way. I assume it's your wife who's in labor. I'll take her and get her situated. While I do, stay here and try to relax. After the doctor finishes examining her and says it's alright, you can come back, but only two people at a time. Everything will be fine. She's in good hands." She did smile at me when she said the last part.

Sean bristled, and I put my hand on his chest. He glanced down at me. I smiled. "Honey, she's right. You've got to calm down."

"I can't. This is something I can't control, Cass. If anything happens to you or our kids, I'll lose my shit," he told me. He didn't yell it, but he was loud enough, the nurse heard. She was close enough that I could read her name badge—*Zia*.

"Zia, pardon my husband and these other big apes. They're just overly protective," I told her with a smile.

She gave me one back and stated, "I understand."

As I studied her, I couldn't help but note how lovely she was. Glancing down at her hand, I checked if she wore a ring, although it wasn't guaranteed she was unmarried if she didn't have one. Her fingers were bare. Hmm, she had a backbone. If she continued to display it, I knew a few guys and even gals back at Patriots' headquarters who might need someone like her. Of course, I wouldn't say anything. Sean teased me enough about playing matchmaker with those who worked for us. Hey, what can I say? I wanted everyone to be as happy as I was.

She smiled at me. "Right this way," she said.

Sean refused to let go of me until he kissed me. And it wasn't a tiny peck on the lips, then go. No, my man kissed me like he wouldn't ever see me again. By the time he let me go, I felt wobbly. Lucky for me, Zia had produced a wheelchair from somewhere, and she had me sit in it. I waved at my clan as she wheeled me toward my room.

When the door to my room closed behind us, she sagged and remarked, "Whew, they're intense. That kiss was something, too. I thought I'd wet myself telling them to behave and getting those glares," she said cheekily. She was helping me to my feet.

"Don't worry. As long as you're not out to harm anyone they love or someone undeserving of being harmed, they won't bite. They're all former SEALs who have the overprotective gene," I assured her.

As she got me changed and into bed, we chatted about ourselves. It was something to fill the time between her questions about my condition. She was seamless about it. Before I knew it, I was in the hospital gown, hooked to monitors, and she was checking my cervix. She nodded her head as she withdrew her hand and removed her gloves.

"You're progressing quickly. You're already at five centimeters. Let me see if Dr. Maggio is here yet. Also, I gotta make sure your guys didn't cause all the other staff to leave," she added as she chuckled, then walked out.

I stared around the room. It was a replica of the one I'd had Noah in. God, in some ways, that felt like it had been forever ago, but in other ways, it felt like it had only been last week.

I recalled that delivery when there was a knock on the door, and then it was opened, and Dr. Maggio and Zia strolled in. I adored him. He was great. Of course, Sean hadn't been thrilled that I had a male doctor when I first saw him when I got pregnant with Noah. He quickly warmed up to him, the same for Mark, Griff, and Gabe. The funny thing was that Dr. Maggio knew their type and got a kick out of them. He was sixty and loved to joke about how their worry made him feel young. He was smiling as he approached the bed.

"Well, look who had to interrupt my beauty sleep. I knew it would happen, too. And then I walk in here to see those four faces glaring at everyone. If all the staff run, I'm holding them responsible," he teased.

"Doc, you know their bark is worse than their bites, or at least in this situation," I reminded him.

"I know. I just love to make them snarl. I told Sean I was coming to check on my sweetheart. He almost blew a gasket." He chuckled, and Zia giggled.

"Are they behaving? I left Gemma and Hadley with them," I asked, almost afraid to find out.

"Those two are trying, but I think they may soon resort to knocking the other four out. Where's Sloan? She needs to keep the big guy controlled," he stated.

"My brother needs to keep himself calm. As for Sloan, she's with the kids. She'll be here later."

"They're intense. Once we get you ready, maybe letting a couple back here will calm them down," Zia offered.

Dr. Maggio and I snorted and muttered, "Not in this lifetime."

They worked swiftly. Dr. M examined me like Zia had, and he nodded once he was sure I was all set.

"I think we're safe to let Sean and whoever in. Try to stay calm. Your water breaking will make you progress quicker. If you start to slow down, we'll do the Pitocin and see what it does. Everything is looking good. I'll be in and out. Zia or one of the others can always get a hold of me. If you need a knockout shot for the four devils out there, I'll see what I can do," he said with a wink, and then he was gone.

"I'll be back," Zia promised before she left.

It felt like no time passed before the door opened again, and in came Sean. On his heels was Mark. I loved Griffin and Gabe, but I loved Mark even more. He was my big brother. He'd looked out for me our entire lives. Sean came to the bed and kissed me on the lips. He was shoved to the side moments later.

"Stop drooling all over my sister. That's how she ended up in this predicament. I should've killed you years ago, and then I wouldn't be exposed to this god-awful sight," Mark grumbled.

Sean elbowed him in the ribs. "As if you could kill me. And you have no one to blame but yourself, Undertaker. That's what happens when you go undercover for five years in a motorcycle club," he reminded him.

My anger over being kept in the dark and left to believe my brother had been dead when he wasn't had mostly eased. Although, at times, it did rear its head. Lucky for them, it wasn't today. Maybe it was because we didn't tiptoe around the subject. What Mark did to save and protect others was incredible. He lost five years of his life due to his sense of honor and duty, but in the end, it led him in a crazy way to meet Sloan, so how could I hold it against him? Seeing him with her and their son made it worth it.

"I know that, but I thought Griff and Gabe would be able to keep you two apart. Now move so I can kiss her," Mark told him.

He was scowling, but I saw the amusement lurking in his eyes. Sean gave a loud, weary sigh and reluctantly moved to allow my brother to reach me. As he hugged me, I couldn't help but flash back to the first time I saw Sean. It was the beginning of us, although, at the time, none of us knew it. It was hard to believe it started nineteen years ago.

Cassidy: Nineteen Years Ago

I was so excited I could barely breathe. Mark was coming home today, bringing his new and closest friends with him. It had been months since I'd seen my big brother. Even though he called occasionally and sent letters, it wasn't the same. I missed him so much that it made me sick to my stomach. Dad tried to help keep my mind off missing him, but he did too. We lived for our calls and letters.

It was just the three of us. Mom had died three years ago. I still missed her. She'd ignored the pain she was having in her stomach and waved it off as gas and constipation rather than going to the doctor to see what it was. Because she didn't, she ended up with a perforated bowel. She hadn't been able to recover from the massive infection it caused, and she died. It had devastated us. She knew there was no hope for her in the end, and before she died, she made Mark promise to go to the Navy as planned. It was her dying wish. She knew how much it meant to him and Dad, who'd served in the Navy. Mark had always wanted to follow in our dad's footsteps. Not even a year later, he did.

My brother wasn't content to be just any sailor. Oh no, he had to be elite, just like Dad. He finished his basic and elite training and was now a Navy SEAL. Most kids my age probably didn't know what that meant, but I did. I'd listened to the chatter at home—even the discussions I wasn't supposed to hear. I knew my dad and brother were badass men. I was proud of them. And I was thrilled they didn't treat me like a nuisance, and I was taught how to do many things most people would say were only to be taught to sons.

I knew the names of the guys he was bringing home with him. He talked about them a lot on our calls and in his letters. They were Gabe, Sean, and Griffin. They were around his age, which made them nine to ten years older than my eleven years. I couldn't wait to meet them. I'd always wanted more siblings. Four older brothers might be overkill, but I'd take it.

"Cass, get down here. Your brother is here," Dad hollered up the stairs.

I ran from my room and pounded down the stairs. I hadn't heard their car. As I came to a halt at the bottom of the steps, I saw four men standing next to Dad. Immediately, I threw myself into Mark's arms. He was in front of the others. He hugged me tightly, lifted me off the ground, and kissed my cheek.

"It's so good to see you, sis," Mark said.

I was choking back tears. I refused to be a crybaby. "It's good to see you, too. It's about time you came home and let Dad see you. He's been a wreck."

This remark earned me chuckles from those around us and Mark. He held me up for another minute before he set me back on my feet. God, I hated being short. I kept hoping to grow to be much taller, but I wasn't holding my breath at five feet two inches. That meant everyone towered over me, especially these guys. Everyone was six feet or taller. My brother turned me to face the guys with him.

"Dad, Cass, these are my best friends that I've told

you about. This is Griffin, and Gabe is next to him. The last one in the back is Sean. Guys, this is my dad, Adam, and my pain-in-the-butt sister, Cassidy." He said the last bit with a grin. I punched him in the side.

"Watch who you call a pain," I told him.

That made his friends laugh. I saw them up close as they shook Dad's hand and mine. I liked what I saw. Sean was the last one to shake my hand. As he did, a strange thought entered my head. He would turn out to be someone very different from Gabe and Griff. Why or how? I had no clue. It was just a feeling. Returning his smile, I let our hands slip apart. Now wasn't the time for acting weird. I wanted them to like me and want to be my brothers, not just Mark's. All the excitement must be messing with my head.

Sean: Chapter 2 - Present

Cassidy was lying in her hospital bed, chatting with her brother. I was sitting on the opposite side of her bed, listening and watching her. God, it seemed unreal that we were about to have our second child. My life had taken a different turn than I'd ever imagined. A turn for the better, without a doubt.

Growing up the way I had, I didn't trust many people. Hell, until I met Gabe, Mark, and Griff, I hadn't trusted more than a handful, and they all seemed to betray me somehow. With those lessons in mind, I entered the Navy unwilling to get close to anyone—or at least not genuinely close. Superficial relationships were fine.

Sure, I was somewhat friendly and hung out with my fellow sailors, but they never got to know the real me. I kept the real Sean well hidden. When I met those three in basic Underwater Demolition/SEAL training, aka BUD/S training, we'd initially got together to help get each other through the rigors of the training. Even with support, most candidates didn't make it. The washout rate was roughly a third within the first three weeks. Overall, only twenty-five percent of those who tried made it. We were all driven for different reasons. As time passed, we discovered we had more things in common and became tighter. By the time BUD/S ended, I considered them brothers in the truest sense of the word.

There was no one I would ever trust more. And over the past two decades, it still held.

The four of us came from different backgrounds. Gabe's was very different from ours, although his difference was more due to what his family was into and the need to hide it from the world. Until recently, no one outside of us knew what his life was like before going into the military. It came out to a select few more when he met his wife, Gemma. He'd played the mafioso part too convincingly.

Griffin had the most traditional family out of all of us. Both of his parents were still alive and a part of his life. Jessie and Graden were terrific people. They welcomed the rest of us as sons. As for Mark, his family life was second to Griff's in terms of being normal, whatever that meant. He lost his mom a few years before we met, but when we became friends, he still had his dad, Adam, and his little sister, Cassidy.

I smiled as I remembered the first time I met her. Mark had brought us home to meet them for the first time. We'd heard a lot about them and vice versa during training and since becoming a team. We'd lucked out and gotten assigned to work on the same SEAL team. It was wonderful to meet them.

I was the least fortunate one in our four-man group when it came to family. I'd grown up fast and lived on the streets a lot. At first, it was as a small child with my mom. She could never seem to get her life together for long. She'd get a job, and we might get into a crappy apartment, but at least we had four walls and a roof over our heads, which was great in our minds. It varied how long it lasted. Eventually, she'd get fired for one reason or another. Or she'd meet a man and think he was the one, and he'd take care of us for the rest of our lives, and she'd quit her job. The men would inevitably move on, and we'd be back to square one.

My mom had me when she was seventeen—an unwed teen mother without a high school diploma. My dad was some guy in high school she had sex with after a football game. He was from another school, so she had no idea who he was other than a first name. Mom hadn't been an outright slut, but she did like guys and sex. I learned that as I got older. She took off when her parents refused to let her stay in their home if she had me. She refused to tell me their names. She said they weren't our family, so there was no need to know. As scattered as she was, I still adored her. Mom died when I was fifteen. From that point onward, I found ways to survive on the streets while fooling the school and local authorities into thinking I had a parent and a home.

Our erratic lifestyle taught me how to take care of myself and how not to be a victim. I was determined to make something of myself one day, so I fought hard to graduate high school. I knew I needed that diploma to do well in this life. Since I was about ten, I'd dreamed of being in the military. As time went by, that dream morphed into becoming one of the biggest badasses possible in the military, a Navy SEAL. I watched everything and read every book I could find about them. I worked to get the grades so the military would take me. After going through boot camp and my military occupation specialty, MOS, training—which was perfect for starting with—I applied for BUD/S.

I became a Navy diver first. Being in the water was part of being a SEAL—Sea, Air, and Land. My diver training taught me how to do a multitude of things underwater—salvaging, repairing, and maintenance, along with submarine rescue and supporting Special Warfare and Explosive Ordnance Disposal. In addition, I was taught how to maintain and repair diving equipment.

I excelled at whatever they threw at me. When I entered BUD/S training, I thought I was more than ready. Boy, I was wrong. I don't think I would've ever survived it if it wasn't for my brothers. We'd been SEALs for about a year when we came home to meet Mark's family. He'd told us about them, and we wanted to meet Adam. He'd been a SEAL in the Navy many years prior. The stories Mark shared intrigued us.

As for his little sister, I had no siblings. None of us did, so it would be new for us to have one, even if she wasn't blood. After meeting them, Gabe, Griff, and I all swore we'd forever watch out for Cassidy no matter what. We promised we'd be there for his dad and her if anything happened to Mark. On the flip side, Mark, Gabe, and I agreed to do the same for Griffin's parents.

Cassidy had been a tiny thing who came running down those stairs that day to greet her brother and us. She was cute, and I instantly felt the need to protect her. Keeping that promise to Mark wouldn't be hard to do. She chattered and smiled the whole time we were there. Our seven days of leave had been full of fun with them and time out and about just us guys. Cassidy had cried when we left, although she made sure to hide so we wouldn't see it. Mark explained she thought it made her too much of a girl to cry in front of anyone.

I got it. The way Adam and Mark treated her wasn't like how most people treated their female child. Yeah, they did have some tendencies toward protecting her, but they were smart and taught her how to take care of herself. She was trained to fight and shoot and various other things that most people equated with skills you taught boys, not girls. Those lessons rolled over to us, and we did the same over the subsequent years.

We visited them and Griffin's parents as often as possible. Cassidy would send us letters, and we'd do so in return. In between, we'd get care packages from her like we did Griffin's parents. Sometimes, we'd all be on a call with her and Adam. As time passed, we grew closer as brothers-in-arms and with our extended family. Then things began to change. The first was when we came home and saw a guy come to the house to take her out on a date. She was sixteen, and the guy was seventeen.

Mark hadn't been happy to find out she was dating. He argued with their dad and her. The rest of us took Mark's side. She was pissed at all four of us, but we didn't care. When the boy came to the door to get her, we stood there trying our hardest to make him run. He'd been nervous, but the fucker remained there and took her out for their date. Cassidy had glared daggers at all of us and threatened to kill us if we didn't stop. Adam appeared amused more than anything, although he had already met the boy and had given him his "if you hurt or touch my daughter, I'll kill you" speech.

We got in my car and went after them as soon as they left. We knew where they were going. Adam insisted on knowing who would be there, where it was, and how late she planned to be out anytime she went on a date. She was to call and inform him if she decided to change anything.

That night, it was dinner and then the movies. We sat outside the restaurant the entire time but could see through a window where they were seated. His every move was watched. Once they got to the movie theater, we hung back until the show was about to start, and then we snuck into the back. It was easy to locate her before the lights went down. She had beautiful strawberry-blond hair, which was eye-catching.

We watched him, not the movie. He had his arm resting along the back of her chair. I wanted to go down and tear off his arm and beat him with it. The others said to wait and see what else he might do. I told them we could kill him if he went to the bathroom, and no one would have to know. Mark agreed with me. Gabe and Griffin were a smidge calmer about it. Didn't they know what that arm behind her back could lead to?

After they left the movie, we continued to follow them. The boy didn't take her straight home. Instead, they went to a secluded spot. One that Mark told us was a favorite make-out spot for people. That's when we revealed ourselves. We tore the driver's door open just as his mouth touched hers. Suffice it to say, by the time we were done scaring the crap out of him, he never asked her out again. Of course, Cassidy had been furious with us, and when we got home, she went off on us. It took a long time to earn her forgiveness for our interference.

A loud hiss had me focusing back on my gorgeous wife. She was grimacing, and her hands were rubbing her stomach. A glance at the machine attached to her stomach told me she was having another contraction. I got to my feet, laid my hands on her rounded tummy, and massaged it. She sighed in relief.

"Breathe. Listen to my voice and breathe in and out. You've got this, Foxy," I told her with a smile.

"I swear to God, Sean, this one is worse than Noah.

He's kicked the hell out of me for months, and now he wants to make it hurt even more. Where the hell is Dr. Maggio with my epidural? It'll be too late to get it if they wait too long. And if I have to go through childbirth without anything for pain, someone will be castrated. Who do you think that'll be?" She growled.

Mark wordlessly handed me a damp washcloth. I took it and placed it on her forehead as he said, "Let me go see where Maggio is. I'll hurry his ass along." He had on his best Undertaker glower. I knew we'd have the epidural placed in no time. He kissed her cheek, gave me a chin lift, and then marched out of the room.

Cassidy weakly chuckled. "He can't stand not to be in control. I hope he doesn't scare the shit out of all the staff who you guys haven't terrified already. You keep it up, and it'll just be us delivering this baby."

"Hey, we can do it. Between all of us, we have enough medical knowledge to deliver a baby."

"We do, but I'd prefer to leave it to the pros. You seemed to be lost in your thoughts over there. Are you alright?"

Leave it to her to worry about me when she was in pain and working so hard to bring our second son into the world safely. Smiling, I leaned over and gave her a kiss. She eagerly returned it. When our lips parted, she sighed.

"I was remembering my life before I met the guys and you. And what happened on that date you went on when you were sixteen, and we were home on leave."

"Don't you remind me! I was mortified, and that poor boy wouldn't even look at me at school after that. He warned all the guys never to go on a date with me. He said I had deranged killers waiting to wipe out anyone who took me out or showed interest in me. Do you know how hard it was to get a date for my senior prom because of you assholes?" She was back to glaring a little.

I grinned. "I know. It gave us time to think up more ways to keep horny boys away from you."

"Yeah, while I had to sit back and know all of you were out screwing whomever you wanted. It killed me."

"Baby, I hate that I hurt you the way I did. If I could go back and change things, I would. I know I fought too long to keep you in the sister role when it wasn't how either of us felt. When you were sixteen, I wasn't ready to see you as being almost a woman. I kept picturing you as the eleven-year-old I first met."

Her mouth opened to respond, but she was cut off by Mark, Dr. Maggio, and Zia, the nurse who'd been steadily taking care of her since we walked in the door.

"Alright, let's get this epidural placed. Just remember, it may slow down your labor. If it happens, we'll administer the Pit to counteract it. I know this is useless to ask, but I will anyway. Will you two wait outside until we're done?" he asked. He gave us an amused look as he did. That changed to a grin when we shook our heads no.

"Alright, Zia, let's get her into position. You know which I prefer. You two, stand back out of the way."

We moved out of his way. He laid out a tray of items. I knew enough from Noah's birth that he was maintaining a sterile field. You didn't want to contaminate the needle going into the spinal area. He put on sterile gloves last. Zia had gotten Cass sitting up on the edge of the bed and had cleansed her back with alcohol and then Betadine. Cassidy was curled over, arching her back. I hated to see her being stuck or to hear her whimper, but she was a champ, and in no time, the epidural was in place, and she was lying down again. Her expression was serene. Maggio tested her sensation before nodding in satisfaction.

"It's good. Zia, tell me the timing of her contractions over the next half hour. If they slow down, I'll tell you how much Pitocin to give her. I know this bunch. They're more than anxious to see this baby born."

"Thanks, Doc," I told him. He waved it off and left.

Zia kept up a flow of chatter as she assessed Cass and made sure she was comfortable. As she did, Mark kissed Cassidy.

"I'm going out and letting someone else come in," he told her.

"Okay, see you later."

"What's it like to have three big brothers and a husband who try to intimidate everyone they see?" Zia asked after he left.

"Mark, the one who just left, is my blood brother. Griffin and Gabe, I inherited along with this one when Mark went to SEAL training."

"You're SEALs?" she asked in surprise.

"We were. We have our own business these days."

"I can't imagine how tough that training was. No wonder you're all so intimidating. Although, you might want to cool it. One of these days, it may get you in trouble," Zia said with a smirk.

Her remark led Cassidy to tell her tales about the four of us. I was trying to defend us when Griff and Hadley walked in. As soon as he saw Zia, he gave it to her straight.

"I know it's supposed to be only two people at a time, but we can't do that, and Doc knows it. I'm her brother, Griffin, and this is my wife, Hadley. You can try to throw us out, but it's not happening."

Zia rolled her eyes and glanced at Cassidy. "I see what you mean. Well, let me say this. You don't scare me, but Dr. Maggio already informed me earlier that you wouldn't follow the rules, and as long as you don't get in the way or cause problems, I'm to ignore it. However, if you do either, I'll have you thrown out. I'm a nurse. I know ways to hurt and kill you that you can't even imagine. Being big bad SEALs doesn't scare me."

His momentary shock morphed into humor, and we all burst out laughing. She grinned, then turned back to Cassidy.

"Try to get some sleep. You're getting closer to the transitional phase. Conserve your energy. Don't talk her to death. She needs to rest up for what's next. Call if you need me. I'll be back in a bit."

We all watched her leave. Glancing at Cass, I saw her eyes droop. She hadn't gotten much sleep before her water broke. Gesturing to Hadley and Griff, we softened our voices. I was so damn ready to meet our son and introduce him to his family. We might not be a typical one, but we were full of love and protection. There was nothing I wouldn't do to keep my happiness.

Cassidy: Fourteen Years Ago

Lying there with part of my family gathered around me, waiting for what would come next, I floated into an exhausted stupor and returned to more of my memories. Back to when I fell for Sean and the years it took to get him to see me. From the moment I met him that fateful day when Mark brought him home that first time, I adored Sean and my other new brothers. I lived for their visits and letters and the rare call when all four would get on the phone to chat with Dad and me.

I kept living in bliss until I turned sixteen. That's when I recognized and acknowledged that while I loved Gabe and Griffin like brothers, my feelings for Sean differed. I had these weird thoughts and dreams for about six months before they came home on leave. It had been a long time since we'd seen them. They planned to spend a week with us after their week with Graden and Jessie. Not only had we gained the boys, as Dad called them, but we gained Griffin's parents, too.

The moment the door opened and they walked into the house, I was struck with how different my reaction was this time to Sean. I found myself checking him out in a purely female-to-male interest way. Up until then, I knew they were all good-looking men. I never told them since they had big enough egos as it was. I knew women threw themselves at them all the time. They didn't talk about it around me, but I listened to conversations with

Dad when they thought I wasn't around.

I knew about sex, even if I hadn't had it yet. I was finding myself interested in boys at school, but not enough to have sex with any of them. There was one I'd allowed to take me out on a couple of dates. I wanted to see if it would go anywhere. Until then, more than a few guys had asked me out, but I wasn't interested. When Pascal, a senior varsity football player, asked me out, I debated briefly and then said yes. He was always nice to me, he was cute, and girls at school would've given anything to have him ask them out. Plus, he wasn't one of the football players who dated and hooked up with every girl he saw.

He and I had two dates before my brothers came home that fateful day, and I devoured Sean with my eyes. I tried hard not to let my interest show. However, the way my heart sped up and my body reacted, I knew something was there. It was undoubtedly one-sided, but still. There was no way a twenty-six-year-old man would be interested in a teenager.

I'd hugged him the same as the other three, but my breasts tingled, my nipples hardened, and I felt myself start to grow slick between my legs when I did. I covertly inhaled his scent as deeply as possible. When he placed a kiss on my cheek, I wished it was on my mouth.

Those feelings and others, which became evident on the first day, had me agreeing to a date with Pascal the next night. I'd initially planned to stay home the whole week so that I wouldn't miss a moment with them. However, my newly acknowledged feelings had me running scared. I should've known they wouldn't react well to me going on a date. Dad hadn't been much better the first time Pascal came to pick me up. It amused me to see how my dad tried to intimidate him.

When they found out I had a date coming, they did everything they could to convince Dad not to let me go. They argued that I was too young to date and that they hadn't checked the guy out. On and on they went. When Pascal arrived, I tried to run to the car to meet him, but they were waiting. It had been a tense and slightly humiliating meeting. Finally, I gave Dad a big enough pleading look. He told us to go.

I should've stayed home. All night, our conversation had been stilted. I knew why I was acting stiff. I was with Pascal, but the only one I could think about was Sean and how much I wished he and I were on a date.

Throughout dinner and then the movie, I worked to shake my crazy thoughts and feelings. It wasn't until we were done with the movie and Pascal suggested we go to enjoy the moonlight that I forced my inappropriate thoughts away. I agreed to go even though I knew it was a common make-out spot. I did it because I thought it would help me forget about Sean.

When Pascal moved in to kiss me, I closed my eyes and went with it. His mouth barely touched mine before I heard a noise, and then he was gone. Opening my eyes, I saw four hulking SEALs glaring at him. They'd opened his door and yanked him out of the car backward. My face burned in mortification. It wasn't due to Mark, Gabe, and Griffin seeing me kissing a guy. No, it was all due to Sean seeing it. The disappointment and anger on his face had cut deep.

There was a big argument before I was escorted to Sean's car and taken home. Pascal was left to get home on his own. Back at the house, there had been a huge fight.

It was me against them, with Dad trying to play neutral, although I knew he wasn't upset they had interrupted our kiss. I'd stayed mad at the guys for most of their visit. When they left, they told me to accept that I would always be their little sister. Hearing Sean refer to me as such tore me up.

Over the next two years, my feelings for him grew despite my efforts to date other guys and deny I felt anything other than sisterly affection for him. I told myself my dreams about him were just normal teenage hormones. Whenever they came home or there was a call, I had to work to avoid appearing tense. Letters from Sean decreased. Eventually, I graduated high school, and they got out of the military. Although they loved the Navy, they decided not to be lifers. They had an idea to create a business. One where they could help those in need and put some of their skills to work in the private sector.

Dad had helped them start the business. He contributed money to it and used some of his connections to help them get a foot in the door with a few people. They were determined to be a paramilitary group that worked in the private sector.

I loved that they were around more, but I also hated it. I found I was constantly waiting to set eyes on Sean. They worked long, exhausting hours, and Dad did too. I was taking college classes, but I helped out when and where they would let me. They soon found they required unassuming operatives, as they called them. Mainly, it was to infiltrate companies who wanted their security tested and then beefed up if necessary. They found I was perfect for that work.

At first, they refused to let me help, but Dad told them I wasn't in danger with what they were doing and that I had skills. In the end, they let me do a few assignments. I loved the work. When Anderson, a former military contact they knew from their SEAL days, came calling, asking them to help with off-the-books work for the US government, they hadn't said no. He was a man they greatly respected, and if they could keep our country and its people safe, they'd do it. No matter whether they were in the Navy or not, they were still patriots and adrenaline junkies.

Other than my unrequited feelings for Sean, life had been going great. Their company, the Dark Patriots, was growing by leaps and bounds. I kept trying to find a guy who would make me forget Sean. Meanwhile, the four of them were not only working but charming the ladies. It made my chest hurt to see him with a woman and know he was sleeping with her.

By the time I was nineteen, I knew it was no use. My feelings for Sean were more than a crush. I'd romantically fallen in love with Sean at sixteen, and nothing would change that. I knew I had to tell him. I prayed that once he knew I felt the way I did, he'd declare that he loved me, too. I'd gotten all dolled up and went to Dark Patriots one night to tell him. I knew he was working late.

I let myself into the building using my badge. The place was dark and quiet. When I got close to his office, I saw his light on. I sped up. I was so nervous but excited, too. I swore the week before that I noted interest on his face when he was at the house. I was almost to the ajar door to his office when I heard moaning. I froze, and as I stood there, I fought not to cry.

"Oh my God, Sean. Yes, touch me there. Jesus. That's it. Please, hurry. I'm close. Damn it," a woman said breathily.

"Patience, Connie. I promise I'll get you off, and then we can get off together. Christ," he muttered.

"I can't believe this is happening," she panted.

"Why not?"

"Well, you're always with Cassidy. I thought there was something between you two. I see the way she looks at you. She loves you, and I think you love her, too."

My face burned with shame, knowing someone knew my secret feelings. I turned from hot to cold when he laughed.

"Come on, do you think I'd go for a girl when I can have a woman? I do love her, but not in that way. Cassidy is like a sister to me, and I'm like her brother. Believe me, I'll never be anything more than that to her. Now, come for me," he said huskily.

As her orgasm hit her and she cried out, I ran out of the building as if my ass was on fire. I cried so hard that it was impossible to see to drive. I ended up pulling over and crying my eyes out. It was hours later before I made it home. I still lived with Dad. He told me it would be a waste for me to move out when he had all that space. I hoped he'd be asleep when I came in. Unfortunately, he hadn't been, and the fact that I'd been crying was evident. He came out of his chair as soon as he saw my face.

"Cassidy, what's wrong? Are you hurt?"

"No, I'm fine, Dad. I'm just tired. I need to get some sleep."

I tried to walk past him, but he hooked my arm and stopped me. "Bullshit. Tell me. You know you can talk to me about anything. Do I have to go out and kill someone? Did someone hurt you or touch you?" he growled.

"No one touched me. I can't talk right now."

"I'm calling the boys."

When he said that, my restraint on my broken heart shattered. "No! I don't want them here. You can't call them."

He reared back in alarm. "Sweetheart, what the hell is going on? If someone hurt you, and I see they have, the boys need to know. We'll make sure the son of a bitch who did pays for it."

"It was my stupidity that got me hurt. I want to forget tonight ever happened, and you have to promise not to tell them."

He shook his head. "I can't promise that unless I know what happened. Were you... assaulted?" he asked hoarsely.

"No, I wasn't raped or beaten."

He sighed in relief. "Okay, then it can't be that bad. Tell me. Come sit with your dear old dad and let me fix whatever it is."

I let him tug me to the couch. He talked for a minute or so, urging me to tell him before I burst into tears and confessed.

"I went to the office tonight. I wanted to talk to Sean. I knew he was working late. I heard a hard truth, and it upset me."

"Sean did this? What did he say?" He frowned.

I ran through the highlights of it. My chest hurt, and tears were streaming down my face again. When I was done, Dad held me and let me soak his shirt with my tears. When I calmed down, he spoke.

"Honey, I know you're in love with Sean. I've known it since you were sixteen. And I know finding him with someone and hearing that hurt but don't give up hope. I believe he loves you and not as a little sister. He's fighting it for some reason. You need to give him time. However, don't pin all your hopes on him either. You're not living. Date, have fun, live. I can't guarantee he'll declare his love one day, but I think there's a good possibility."

We'd sat up late into the night talking. In the end, I was determined to do as Dad said. At the time, I had no idea that would be the last time we'd talk about me and Sean. A month later, Dad dropped dead from a stroke. After that, I was left in a daze. The five of us continued to go through the motions of everyday life, but I was in agony. Not only was Sean not reciprocating my feelings, but I didn't have my beloved father to make me feel better. I couldn't talk to Mark or the other two about my feelings. They wouldn't understand. Life limped along.

Eventually, I slowly began to live, although Mark and the guys kept trying to smother me. I tried to stay away from Sean as much as I could. I knew my standoffishness was causing worry, but every time I saw him with a woman, I felt like I'd been stabbed. Before I knew it, three years had passed. That's when my life was torn apart again. Mark was on an assignment I knew nothing about. I found out when the plane he was on went down, and he was killed. Once again, my world shattered, and I knew I was on borrowed time.

Sean: Chapter 3 - Four-and-a-Half Years Ago

As Cassidy slept, I thought back to when it all had come full circle for us. It was hard to believe it had only been four-and-a-half years. I shuddered as I recalled how close I came to missing out on this. My damn hardheadedness was almost my undoing. I'd been so damn adamant that I had to remain a brother to her rather than a lover that I damn near destroyed us and our chance at happiness. I loved her and our children more than anything in the world. I might not have met Nash yet, but I instantly fell in love with him the moment she told me she was pregnant again.

Looking back with a clear head, I knew I began to acknowledge Cassidy was a woman when she turned eighteen, but I didn't want to. I fought against it. Hell, even when she was sixteen, there was no denying she was almost one. I kept telling myself she was a girl and nothing more than a sister. I dated and fucked women in countless attempts to kill the feelings I had growing for her. I kept telling myself my feelings for her weren't right. Adam and Mark trusted me to be there for her as a brother and friend, not her lover. When they died, I told myself they'd come back to haunt me if I tried anything. That thinking caused me to remain in my hell, and I watched as she went on with her life and dated other men. I wanted to kill every single one of them.

Things were never the same after we lost Adam. It steadily grew worse until we lost Mark. His death gutted us all. We were in agony when he was presumed dead in that plane crash. We contemplated selling the business because the thought of carrying on with it without him didn't sit right. I wanted to comfort Cassidy in every way imaginable, but I kept telling myself it was wrong. If only I'd told Mark what I felt for her before he died and had gotten his blessing, then things might've been different.

One of the largest daggers to my heart during that time was I suspected she loved me. I saw how she cared for me and looked at me when she thought I wasn't looking. Griff and Gabe told me she did. They demanded I stop being foolish and tell her. I didn't. Not even after the three of us found out a year after his supposed death that Mark was alive and working undercover to take down one of the largest outlaw motorcycle clubs in the country. For the next couple of years, I used the excuse that I didn't want to endanger him by diverting his attention by telling him of my feelings for his sister. As if that wasn't enough, I was lying to her about him being dead. I feared what she'd say and do when she found out.

It all came to a head on that fateful mission we ran with the Warriors MC in Dublin Falls—one I had been determined Cassidy wouldn't participate in. After Adam's and Mark's deaths, we stopped using her for missions we felt were too high-risk. The reason was simple—we couldn't risk losing her, too. If she got hurt or killed, it would be the end of the three of us, especially me.

In true Cassidy fashion, she thumbed her nose at us and went to work with another agency that did work kinda along the lines of what we did, but not the covert military missions we did for Anderson and others. It could still be dangerous. We tried to get her to quit. We even tried to force the other company to fire her, but they refused. Having to allow her to join us on the Warriors' mission to take down the traffickers selling women in the Middle East had terrified me. But we had no choice. The operative we planned to use was unavailable. She'd broken her leg.

After we got to the Warriors' compound, my feelings had to be glossed over, although not forgotten. I fought hard not to lose my mind and inflict damage when I had to watch several bikers watch her with interest in their eyes. Who could blame them? She was sexy, drop-dead lovely, and damn intelligent. Any man would be blessed to have her as his. As if seeing multiple guys eyeing her wasn't enough for my tattered restraint, I had to watch her laughing and spending time with one of them over the others. She was smiling, joking, and hanging out with Falcon.

One night in particular came to mind. We'd gotten into it several times at the Warriors' compound. I'd verbally attacked her about Falcon and what she was doing with him and possibly others, to no avail. I was so crazy jealous, and afraid that I went too far. And I discovered I had when she let me have it. Words had been exchanged at the shooting range earlier that day. It was nighttime, and I was itching to fight and force Cassidy to stop being with him. Hell, to this day, I still don't know what I was thinking when I did what I did.

As usual, the club bunnies would arrive late at night after the children and most old ladies had left. In the past, I'd seen how it worked. I'd even contemplated going there before. This visit, despite what it might look like, I didn't sleep with any of them. I was over trying to use other women to forget my desire for Cassidy. Christ, I couldn't recall a woman I had slept with since finally acknowledging Cassidy held my heart, who didn't make me sick to my stomach to kiss and have sex with. I kept up a good front, but it had been ages since I'd slept with someone. My hand was my only sexual partner. By that point, I was almost sure I'd die alone. I couldn't have her, so what was the point?

I wanted to scream when I saw Josie coming toward me. She wore a determined look. When that determined bunny reached me, she wrapped an arm around my waist, hugged me close, and pressed her tits into my arm. If she thought it would tempt me, she was wrong. I should've left before they came.

However, at that moment, I was hit with a foolish idea. One that would use Josie to make Cassidy jealous and declare that she wanted me, not Falcon or any of the other Warriors. Even if we couldn't be together, I didn't want her with anyone else. I know. It was twisted logic. The idea flickered to life within seconds, and then I acted. I quickly glanced over to see if Cass was watching. She was, and she wasn't happy. I looked back at Josie, wrapped my arm around her, and leaned down to whisper in her ear. I ensured I was smiling, although I only asked her, "What do you think you're doing, touching me?"

Loud gasps made me look over at Cass. When I did, absolute fury hit me. Falcon had her plastered to him, and he kissed her like he was starving. To make matters worse, Cassidy was kissing him back. A growl slipped out of me. Griffin and Gabe moved closer to me. I noted it on a very distant level. I was about to go across the room and tear that fucker's head off when they stopped kissing.

Cass looked over at me, smiled, and then waved. Falcon laughed, took her hand, and began to head for the hall where his room was. What broke my restraint was when he put his hand on her plump ass and squeezed it. I pushed Josie away and went after them. Gabe and Griff grabbed me, but I shook them off. Catching up to them, I grabbed Falcon by the shoulder and spun him around to face me.

"Get your fucking hands off her, Falcon," I growled before looking at her. "Why in the hell are you acting like this, Cass? You're acting like a pissed teenager trying to get back at a parent. Sleeping with him doesn't prove anything other than you're acting like a slut."

More gasps were heard around the room. I wanted to groan. I knew I said the wrong thing. No one would ever accuse Cassidy of being a slut. *Shut up, stupid!* I lectured myself to no avail.

Cassidy's face flushed with anger. "Look who's calling someone a slut. How many of the bunnies have you banged here, Sean? Don't you ever call me a slut. I don't sleep around just to get off, unlike you and most guys. My relationship with Falcon isn't any of your business. I can spend time with him or anyone else in whatever capacity I deem appropriate. That includes fucking them. I've had enough of this shit. You've made it abundantly clear that you want me to stay away."

I felt sick seeing the tears in her eyes. Before I could say anything, she continued. "I get it. You don't like me or want me. You feel responsible for me because Mark asked you to watch out for me. Well, I'm over it, and you. You'll be glad to hear that it will no longer be necessary or even possible. As soon as this mission ends, I'm moving the hell out of Virginia. I'm going somewhere you can't drop in any time you please. You're a hypocrite, Sean. You don't live life. You close yourself off. I've been waiting for you to admit you had feelings for me all these years. You refuse, going so far as to throw other women in my face. No more. How does it feel? Oh, and for your information, I haven't slept with Falcon, but that changes tonight! Goodnight, Sean."

She turned her back on me, and Falcon smirked and went with her. I was frozen, trying to digest what she said, but their walking off rattled me into responding. I tried to go after them, but the others stopped me. I had no choice but to shout after them.

"Cass, don't you dare fucking sleep with him! That's just spiteful."

"That's rich coming from Mr. Spiteful himself. Fuck you, Sean. I'm done. Once we're done with this, stay away. I don't want to see you again."

I roared out my pain as they disappeared down the hallway and stormed outside. I knew if I stayed, I'd kill him. I spent hours that night walking, driving around in the dark, and working through my thoughts. In the end, I knew I only had myself to blame for her sleeping with him. I pushed her away one time too many. Despite how it gutted me to know he had her, I knew I'd do anything to make her stay in Virginia and work out our differences. I resolved to start on it the following day.

Only she made sure to keep us from being alone for the remainder of our time at the compound. It was god-awful when Everly and she allowed themselves to be taken at that Gala. Spending the subsequent days biding our time, not knowing what might be happening to her and Everly had cut even deeper. I lived in absolute terror. There was no guarantee they wouldn't be raped or killed.

Just because the rumor was they didn't touch the women they took due to greed and desire to get the best price, there was no assurance it wouldn't happen. Even when we got ears inside, and we were outside, it wasn't enough. Smoke and I were miserable together.

I knew I was done when we stormed that building after the auction to rescue them and the other women being held there. There would be no more running from or denying my feelings. I loved Cassidy and would do everything I could to make her mine. I had a shit ton to make up for. I didn't care how long it took. I'd find a way to make it up to her and win back her love.

I kept telling myself she still loved me. That Falcon was merely a fling and her way of hurting me. That was the plan, but Cassidy wasn't cooperating at all. Man, she'd fought me tooth and nail to remove me from her life. Recalling the return trip and the subsequent disappearing act she pulled, I slid further into my memories as she rested.

We rode back together to Hampton. It was where we all lived and where the office of the Dark Patriots was located. It was just over five hundred miles, so it was a good eight hours of driving without stops to gas up, grab something to eat, or take bathroom breaks. She sat in the backseat, staring out the window. I was with her. Griff and Gabe kept jerking their heads and glancing toward her from the front seat. It was clear they wanted me to talk to her.

"Nice job on the mission. You and Everly did great. It seemed like you two made a friend with Bryony. I sure hope she and those other women get the help they need. I wouldn't wish what they went through on anyone," I told her. She barely glanced at me, shrugged, and went back to staring out her window.

"Cass, I know you must be tired after all that. Why don't you snuggle in and take a nap? Use Sean's lap as a pillow. We've got a few hours before we have to stop. You barely slept in there, although who could blame you," Griffin suggested.

"I'm fine, Griff. I don't need to sleep. I have so much to think about and organize in my head. All I'd do is dream and drift. I'll sleep later once I'm home."

"What are you thinking about?" Griff asked.

"What do you need to organize?" Gabe asked at the same time. I waited impatiently to hear her answer.

"My life. It's time I figure out where I want to live. Dad's house needs to be sold, and I need to pack. Oh, and I have to talk to my bosses to see if they're alright with me working from a different state. I don't see why not. Others do it."

"What the hell do you mean? Figure out where you want to live! You love your house. Jesus Christ, what's gotten into you?" Gabe asked incredulously.

"As long as I hang onto memories and silly dreams that will never come true, I'll never be happy. I talked to Everly and made the decision. I need a clean break. Selling and moving will help with that."

Gabe whipped the car off the road onto the berm and came to a hard stop. He threw the gearshift into park and then spun partway around to stare at her in shock and anger. Griff was doing the same.

"You leaving your family and everything familiar isn't the answer. If you're unhappy, figure out why and change it." He sneaked a peek at me.

"I can't breathe. You guys try to dictate my life, both personal and professional. I can't even·work at your company because you refuse to use my talents. You want me to sit on my ass in the office all day. That's not me. I know Mark and Dad asked you to look out for me, and I appreciate it. But I'm grown up. I can take care of myself. I'm twenty-five years old. It's time to have fun and go wild. In a few years, if things work out, I might settle down and have a family. To be able to do that, I can't be near you guys."

Her remarks about having fun and going wild made my head pound. All I could imagine was her in bed with Falcon or some other faceless man. Make that several faceless men. "You're not leaving Virginia," I stated loudly.

"Where are you planning to go?" Griff asked.

"I'm not sure. I thought of California, Texas, or who knows. I'll have to do some research."

"How are we supposed to see you if you're that far away?" Gabe asked.

"That's the beauty of it. You can't. I'm done living this life. You've all fulfilled your promise to my brother and dad. You protected me. I can take it from here."

Her jaw was set determinedly. I reached out and captured one of her hands. She tried to pull it away, but I held tight. "Cassidy, you're not leaving your home. You're tired and not thinking clearly. Let's just get you home and rested, and then you and I need to talk."

She studied me, then shook her head and turned back to the window. I wasn't sure what it meant, but as the miles sped by, I continued to organize what I would say to her as soon as she recovered from the ordeal. I'd give her time to get over it, and then we'd sit down and talk. I tried to hang onto her hand, but she eventually yanked it free. I felt cold inside as we got closer to

Hampton.

❧❧❧

After getting back to Hampton and Dark Patriots headquarters, we were hit with a ton of things that needed to be taken care of right away. Not only were we still cleaning up the human trafficking mess, but we also had numerous other projects and missions requiring our attention. The three of us worked with many of our staff from six in the morning to midnight. They didn't mind receiving overtime.

I was desperate to talk to Cassidy about her moving and us. I had to make her see that we were meant for each other. I was done denying I loved her and knew she loved me. I might've battered her love some, but I refused to believe it had died. She was hurt and lashing out. I couldn't blame her. However, all attempts in the short breaks in my hectic schedule to get her to come and see me were shot down. She always had an excuse. Most of them pertained to her job. She was working on several assignments. If it wasn't that, she claimed to be too exhausted to meet. Like an idiot, I let her slide.

It had been two weeks, and there was light at the end of our relentless work schedule. I was taking time for myself this afternoon, and I knew exactly what I would do with it. I'd told Griff and Gabe I was going to see Cassidy. Recalling their response, I rolled my eyes. Facing my brothers across my desk, I told them I would be unavailable unless it were an emergency.

"I'm headed out in about an hour. I won't be back today. If an emergency happens, call me. Otherwise, I'm unavailable."

"Oh yeah, where are you headed?" Gabe asked.

"I'm headed over to see Cassidy. She and I need to

talk."

"Are you planning to lecture her, or are you finally getting your head out of your ass and manning up?" Gabe asked.

"What do you mean, manning up?"

"You know what he means. Christ, Sean, we're your best friends and brothers, but you've fucked around long enough. If you don't tell Cass how you feel about her and want to be with her, you'll lose her for good. You saw her in Dublin Falls. She's at the breaking point. You heard her talk about moving and selling the house. I'm scared to death we'll never see her again. Mark is depending on us to keep an eye on her," he hissed. The three of us were still the only ones who knew he was alive. This MC case was dragging on way too long.

"I know all that. And yes, I will tell her I love her and can't live without her. She wants out of that house. She can move in with me. I want her to wear my rings and sleep in my bed every night. No one can love or protect her like I can," I declared.

"Thank God! It's about time. I thought Gabe and I would end up kidnapping the two of you and locking you up until you both came to your senses. Don't just stand there. Go. Get on your knees and beg that woman to put us all out of our misery," Griff exclaimed.

I stood up. "Good luck," Gabe said. Giving them both a chin lift, I didn't waste time getting to the garage or in my car. The drive to her house, the one she grew up in, seemed to be twice as long.

An eerie feeling hit my gut when I pulled up to the house. It was the middle of the day. Most of her neighbors would still be at work. Margie, our receptionist slash assistant, told me Cass worked from home today.

The garage was closed. The street was abnormally quiet. Getting out, I went to the front door and knocked. When I got no answer, I rang the doorbell and knocked again— still nothing. Making a decision, I took out my keys. Gabe, Griff, and I had a key to the house, just as Mark and Cass had them to our homes. Unlocking it, I walked inside, calling her name.

"Cassidy, it's Sean. Where are you? We need to talk, babe. It's past time."

The silence was all I got in return. Shutting the door, I rushed from room to room. Nothing. It wasn't until I got to her bedroom that I knew how badly I'd fucked up. Her dresser drawers were pulled out, and the closet doors hung open. They were bare. She was gone. Fuck! Now, to find her. Back to Dark Patriots to find my woman and bring her home.

Cassidy: Chapter 4 - Four-and-a-Half Years Ago

Everly's house in Florida was beyond lovely. It had a pool. And if I wanted the ocean and sand, it wasn't far to walk to the beach. My decision to leave Virginia had been hard, but it was necessary. If I didn't, I'd spend the rest of my life pining for a man who didn't want me. I'd taken all the hits and dents to my dignity that I could stand. If I didn't get out now, I'd lose the last bit of respect I had for myself.

I had to sneak to do it, but I'd been here a week. I made it appear that I was still in Virginia when, in actuality, I was already in Florida. Everly had helped me out. I was settling in nicely, I thought. Her place was fully furnished, so there was no need to move my furniture. I knew, eventually, I'd have to return to pack up the house and sell it, but for now, this was perfect. I packed as many boxes of clothing and personal stuff as my car could carry and then hit the road.

I also lucked out on the job front. My bosses had no issue with me working from there. In fact, they loved it. They seemed to get a lot of business in Florida. It was a seamless transition to a local office they kept there. I was fully trained so I could hit the ground running. I arrived on a Saturday, and by Monday, I was at work.

You'd think with everything falling into place the way it was, I'd be happy. I wasn't, but I was determined to be. In an effort to make the transition and get started on the task of forgetting Sean, I agreed to go out for drinks with a guy in the office. He'd been friendly from the moment he met me. He showed me around the office and told me he'd be glad to show me the sights once he knew I hadn't been to Florida before.

The old me would've turned him down and wallowed in my misery that Sean didn't love me. The new me had vowed to do the opposite—no more hiding. So I said yes when he asked if I'd go out on Friday night to have drinks with him and listen to music at a local bar. It was date night, so I went home to get ready after work. He offered to pick me up, but I was more comfortable meeting him there. That way, I could leave if I wanted, and he wouldn't know where I lived.

It was April, and the weather was warmer than I was used to. We were still probably getting snow, ice, and rain back home. With the difference in mind, I dressed in a favorite outfit of mine. I wore black tights and boots that molded my lower legs, coming to below my knees. They had a decent heel on them—three inches. I paired them with a skirt. It was black as well and hugged my hips. It hit mid-thigh. A wide belt cinched in my waist, and my top was a faux turtleneck in a dark green. I loved how it set off my green eyes. I wore my hair down, and my makeup was tasteful but heavier than I usually wore it during the day. With my jewelry on, I was feeling pretty and confident.

I drove to the bar and got there in plenty of time to check it out. I might not be living with the guys nearby, but the lessons they, my dad, and Mark had taught me weren't forgotten. By the time I took a seat inside to wait for Travis, I knew where the exits were, who was the most likely to pose a danger if they popped off, and who I might be able to count on in an emergency. Those were skills all of them had taught me. Realizing I was thinking of them, I pushed those thoughts away. If I could think of all but him, I would, but it wasn't possible. It's why I had to leave them all behind.

It was five 'til seven when my date came strolling through the door. I liked a man who could be on time or even early. Score one point for him. He was scanning the bar. I stood and waved my hand so he could see me. When he saw me, a huge smile spread across his face. He made his way to me. When he reached me, he snagged one of my hands and raised it to his lips to kiss it as he examined me.

"Wow, I didn't think it was possible, but you look even more stunning than you do during the day. How can that be? I hope you haven't been waiting long or been subjected to a bunch of men hitting on you." He frowned a tiny bit as he scanned the people surrounding us.

The bar was filled with high-top tables and a long line of stools. It was a very popular place if the crowd was anything to go by. I'd gotten lucky and found us a two-seater high table.

"Thank you, that's quite the compliment. I hope this is alright. There isn't much selection in this section. You look dashing tonight. It's always fun to see how people dress and act outside of work." We both took our seats. I was pleased that he moved my chair back to allow me room to sit and then pushed it closer to the table after I did.

"It is. You learn so much more about each other. Did

you have any trouble finding it?"

"Nope."

I watched as he flagged down a waitress. When she stopped, we gave her our orders. Since I was out alone, I would have only one alcoholic drink and then stick to water or carbonated beverages. I had to drive, and there was no way I would be inebriated. I was more of a sweet and fruity drinker than a whiskey or bourbon gal. I did like tequila, so I ordered a Tequila Sunrise. It was made up of three ingredients—tequila, orange juice, and grenadine. Travis ordered a Jack & Coke.

As we waited, he began to ask me questions. They weren't invasive or anything. They were the standard ones someone asked when they were getting to know someone.

"Where exactly did you come from? I know you said you're not a native Floridian."

"I'm not. I grew up and lived my whole life in Virginia, near the coast."

"If you don't mind me asking, why did you move? I mean, I love it here, but Virginia is lovely too. I enjoyed it when I visited a couple of years ago."

"I needed a change. I was stagnated living there. I lost my brother a few years back, and several years before, my dad passed away. Everything reminds me of them. I still lived in my family home. I realized I needed a total change of scenery and pace to be happy. A friend was nice enough to offer me the use of her house down here. I worked for another branch of the company, making it easy to transfer."

He reached over and took my hand, squeezing it. "I'm sorry about your dad and brother. I know what it's like not to have a family. I'm all alone, too. We have more in common already."

I smiled and nodded. As time passed, we got to know each other. He was easy to talk to and courteous. I laughed several times. He articulated himself well, and no one looking at him would ever say he wasn't good-looking. While I found him amusing and had a good time, there was no spark. I tried to force it, but it wasn't happening. We spent about three hours in the bar before I had to call it a night.

"Travis, I hate to go, but it's been a long week, and I need my rest. I enjoyed tonight. It's nice to get to know you and make a friend."

His smile slipped away when I referred to him as a friend. We'd risen from our seats and walked toward the bar door. I was suddenly tired. All I wanted to do was go home and sleep after I took a long hot bath.

"Cassidy, we got on great. I don't see us being in the friend zone. I know I don't want that. You're a gorgeous, intelligent woman I want to see again and not as friends. What would you say to that?" he asked.

I had to think for a minute. My heart was hollering that Travis wasn't Sean while my brain was screaming back. *Damn right, he's not! It's time to get on with life and forget him. All he does is hurt you.* My anger at myself for already sabotaging what might be a chance at something good pushed me to smile back and tell him a white lie.

"I would say that another date is definitely in order. How about we talk about it on Monday at work? We can decide where to go and when. I'm still getting situated here, but if I don't have to work too early the next day, no problem," I said, sounding chipper.

My answer put a smile back on his face. It had cooled off outside and was dark. He had his arm around me, escorting me to where the cars were parked. I pointed to my car. He guided me to it and then stopped. He took my key fob and unlocked it. Before opening the door, he stepped closer and lowered his head.

"I hope this isn't too forward, but I've been dying to kiss you since the moment I saw you at work," he said softly before his lips landed on mine.

It was a thorough kiss, but he didn't try to shove his tongue down my throat. He didn't slobber or do anything I could object to. It was all more than okay, but it didn't do a thing for me. I didn't grow warm, my body didn't tighten, and I didn't have images of him and me naked on a bed. When he broke the kiss, I hid my disappointment. *It's only a first date. You don't fall for someone instantly. Give him a chance.*

I smiled at him as he backed away and opened my door. He held on to me until I was settled in the seat. "I'll see you on Monday. Drive safe," he said before closing my door.

I started it and drove away in a contemplative mood. I didn't speed or drive recklessly but was upset when I made it home without remembering the drive. Letting myself into the house, I vowed to work at getting to know Travis and seeing if we had things in common we could build into a relationship. *God, please. Help me forget Sean.*

❦❦❦

Early the following morning, a phone call flipped me from a good mood into a bad one. I was up early getting breakfast when my phone startled me. I hurried over to the counter to see who it was. I groaned when I saw it was Sean's number. A huge part of me wanted to pretend not to be here and let the phone ring. However, I knew how stubborn he could be. He'd keep calling until he drove me mad. Taking a deep breath as I realized the time had come, I answered it. I infused happiness in my voice.

"Good morning, Sean."

"Like hell, it's a good morning," he barked.

"Well, someone got up on the wrong side of the bed. Maybe you should go back to sleep and try again. It's the weekend. You should try to relax."

"I don't need any more goddamn sleep. Tell me where you are," he snapped.

Crap, he'd figured out I left. I played it cool anyway. "I'm at home. Where are you?"

"Fuck if you're at home. I'm looking at your house right now, and you're nowhere to be found. Your clothes and other personal shit are gone. Tell me where you are, and I'll come get you," he snapped.

One of the things I learned from working with the four of them and Dad was how to safeguard yourself. Most people could be tracked using their phones. The movies that showed turning it off were somewhat correct. Sometimes, it did, but if you got an encrypted one, the likelihood of it being traceable was slim to none. We all used them due to the nature of the work we did. Before I left, I got a new one. I didn't put it past them to try and track me. I had calls and texts forwarded to the new one via another encrypted route. Eventually, they would know where I was, and I'd have to face them.

"I'm afraid that isn't possible. I told you, Sean. It's time for me to get a life. Living there in Hampton is killing me. Did you call to yell at me, or did you have a reason? I'm on my way out the door. You have five minutes."

Hearing his voice made my chest ache, and I

wanted to cry and beg him to love me. I forced myself to grow a backbone. Breaking away was the only way. It would be too much, even if I only saw the other two.

"Cass, baby, you can't do this? How do you expect me to stand living apart from you? Not knowing if you're alright will kill me, us. You could be hurt, and I'm not there. Tell me where you are, and I'll come to you. We need to talk. I swear the last thing I want to do is fight." There was an edge of something to his voice.

"Sean, there's nothing more to say. It's done. I moved, and this is for the best. I have a secure place to stay and a job, and I've already begun to make friends. I told you I intended to leave Virginia. The way I was living wasn't healthy. It's time to be on my own. Your promises to Dad and Mark have been more than fulfilled. I'm all grown up and ready to have a family. Here, I can have that."

"A family of your own? What the fuck? Are you with Falcon?" he snarled.

I wanted to lie and say yes for a second, but I wouldn't bring Falcon into the middle of our mess any more than I already had. Falcon had been great about helping me at the Warriors' compound, but his efforts to make Sean admit he loved me and not as a sister had backfired. Sean hadn't declared himself.

"No, I'm not with Falcon."

"Are you with someone else? Are you seeing someone?"

I didn't deny or confirm it. I remained quiet.

"Cassidy, don't. Just let me come to you, and we'll talk. Please." I caught what sounded like panic in his tone, but that couldn't be right. Nothing made him panic. He was just worried he was failing at being a big brother.

"Sean, no, I can't. A clean break is the only way. I've got to go. Goodbye. Be happy," I said quickly at the end before hanging up. Tears escaped my eyes. Immediately, my phone rang again. Knowing I had no choice, I blocked his number.

Needing to get and stay busy so I wouldn't sit there and cry all day, I started on my laundry. It wasn't a lot, but it was something to do. I barely had a load in the washer when my phone rang. Glancing at it, I groaned. It was Gabe. I hesitated, but in the end, I answered.

"Hello, Gabe. Let me guess. Sean told you to call me. Well, I'm not telling you or Griff where I am either, so don't ask."

He chuckled. "You got it, he did, but I'm not asking. I wanted to see if you're alright. I hate that you felt you had to leave, though."

"Gabe, you know why I had to. I can't do it. Seeing you and Griff means seeing him. And I can't be near him, treated like a sister, and watch him with countless women anymore. I want a life. I want and deserve someone to love and have a family with. He can't give those to me. I've finally accepted it. In fact, I met someone, and who knows, we might be able to have something if I give him a chance," I brazenly told him. It was pretty presumptuous after one date and one without a single spark, but I was trying to put positive juju in the air.

He sighed. "I really thought after the mission with the Warriors, he'd accepted his feelings for you, and it would change. He was so damn worried about you, we all were, but him even more. The way he wouldn't let you out of his sight after the rescue made me think he would finally do it."

"See, that's where you and Griff are wrong. He's never loved me, not that way. You kept telling me he did, and he was fighting it. No, he isn't. At most, he loves me as a sister. At the least, he feels an obligation to watch over me. I refuse to be an obligation. I'm sorry, but it means I have to leave the two of you. It's the way it has to be."

"Will you tell us where you are? I swear, we won't tell him. We need to know you're safe, and we'll visit you since coming here is too much."

"Eventually, I will, but not yet. I'm settling in and getting used to it here. I promise, soon, I'll let you know. I love you, and I love Griff. Tell him that, but please, no calls for Sean. I don't want to block you too."

"Okay, we won't. Love you. Talk soon. If you need anything, we're just a phone call away. Be safe."

"I love you too. Be safe."

Hanging up, I was back to being teary-eyed, but I shoved it away. Staying in the house wasn't the answer. I decided to go out and explore the area. I had whole new haunts to create. Changing my clothes and brushing my hair, I was out the door ten minutes later.

❧❧❧

Another week zoomed by. I'd been in my new home for two weeks and quickly learned about the areas near the house and work. After the call with Sean and Gabe last weekend, I talked to Everly on Sunday. She assured me there was no way anyone working for the Dark Patriots could track me. She was doing something to hide my digital footprints. I asked her what would happen if Sean asked Smoke to do it. She laughed and said if Smoke knew what was good for him, he wouldn't.

Work was easy since I'd already been doing it for the same employer. I spent most of the week out of the office working a case, so it meant I hadn't said hello to Travis more than in passing. He texted a couple of times asking how I was, and I replied but explained I didn't have time to chat but would soon.

I wasn't blowing him off, per se. I was second-guessing if I should go out on another date with him. Would I be leading him on if I went a second time? But would I lose out on a possible spark with him if I didn't? It was sort of driving me crazy. All the back and forth had come to an end today. I was in the office, and he point-blank asked me to go on another date tomorrow night. I forced myself to say yes. I would see what I felt after this one and then decide whether this had a chance. If not, I'd let him know we could be friends, but that was it. He appeared pleased when I said yes.

Hours later, I was on the couch watching a movie. I was yawning but trying to stay awake until the end. It was a battle. I struggled and sighed when the credits began to scroll by. Getting up, I shut off the television and went to the bedroom. I completed my nightly ritual of brushing my teeth, face, and hair and then slathered on face and body lotion before getting into bed. I barely turned off the light when I snapped to attention.

I'd become familiar with the outdoor sounds around the house. It was something else I'd been taught. Any changes could signal danger or at least the need to investigate. For example, the next-door neighbor had a dog who stayed outside at night. He was good and didn't bark unless he noted someone in his or the neighbors' yards on either side. I found it out one night when he was barking, and I went to see what was wrong. His owner had explained he'd unexpectedly gone into the backyard in the dark and didn't call out to him, so the dog alerted.

He was the one to assure me that Gus would only bark if there were someone around who shouldn't be.

I took him at his word and hadn't heard another sound from Gus until now. Slipping out of bed, I slid the gun I kept under my pillow out and tiptoed out of my room to the back slider. It was dark outside, but you could make out shadows if you strained enough. Luckily, the neighborhood wasn't one with many streetlights on it. Silently, I undid the alarm and slid the slider open just enough to squeeze out. Gus was still barking, so I headed toward the fence, which separated me from him.

Hank's house was dark, which meant he was either not home or was careful not to alert an intruder that he was aware of them. As a former police officer, Hank knew how to handle a situation like this. I'd shared with him that I worked in security and that I was armed in case there was ever an issue.

I wanted to swear. I was five foot three, and the fence between us was six feet tall. There was no way to see over it unless I found something to stand on. I was running through a list of items in the backyard that I could easily move and use to do that when I heard feet running. However, they weren't coming from Hank's yard. They were coming from mine! Swinging toward where I thought the sound was coming from, I took off. I saw a shadow moving. Running faster, I weaved around the furniture. I heard a curse, then nothing. Coming up along the side where the gate wasn't, I saw the shadow jump up and haul itself over the fence into the front yard.

I usually could do that if I had shoes, but I was in bare feet and a pajama short set. "Fuck," I muttered, then changed direction.

I knew it was futile, but I ran back into the house,

through it, and out the front door. The rev of a car engine and taillights were all I saw as a car sped away. I wouldn't shoot at it. What if I was wrong? As I watched it go, I heard movement to my left. Swinging that way, I relaxed.

"Whoa, it's me, Hank. It seems like someone wanted to commit a late-night robbery. Did they gain access?"

"No. I went to see what was setting off Gus and heard someone running. Whoever it was, he was in my yard and jumped the fence. When I got out here, all I saw was a car leaving."

"There has been a rash of robberies the past few weeks in several areas nearby. This is the first in ours. Come on, let's get you inside, and I'll look around to ensure nothing was disturbed or he gained access through an unlocked window or something."

I didn't bother to tell him that wasn't likely. I kept the alarm set and checked windows every time I came home. Sighing, I led him back inside. Why did people have to rob others? Had whoever it was cased the house earlier, knowing Everly was no longer here, and come back to rob it tonight? It was a distinct possibility. Hopefully, they would be too scared to do it again.

Sean: Chapter 5

I was about to lose my mind. It had been two weeks since I spoke to Cassidy, and I was no closer to knowing where she was than I was then. Talking to her neighbors revealed that she'd left a week before my call to her. I kicked myself repeatedly for not manning up and talking to her as soon as we got back from that assignment in the Middle East. If I had, she'd still be here, and I'd be with her.

Her words about having a life and family had cut deep. Her blocking of my calls hurt more. Gabe and Griffin admitted they'd talked to her a few times., but she refused to tell them where she was. When I pushed them to call for me, they refused. They told me it was my damn fault she'd left. I'd been an asshole long enough. I needed to find and go after her if I wanted her.

Whatever she was doing, she was effectively hiding herself. I tried to get our computer people at the office to trace her, but they couldn't. Unless she'd gained skills I knew nothing about, I realized she was getting help hiding, leading me to stand outside the front door of Smoke and Everly's house on the Dublin Falls Warriors' compound. I was here to talk to Everly. They were the only ones skilled enough to hide her.

The door opened to my knock, and Smoke gestured for me to enter. He didn't seem surprised to see me, although I hadn't told anyone I was coming. I didn't want to give Everly a chance to leave. I should've known she wouldn't, and she would know I was coming. I followed him wordlessly to the kitchen. Everly was sitting at the table with her laptop out. She was staring hard at me.

"Sorry for barging in like this, but I need to talk to you. Everly, you know why I'm here," I stated boldly. Smoke was quiet and came closer to listen.

"I do? Why would I?" she asked innocently.

I scowled at her. She was going to make me say it. "Because you and Smoke are the only two capable of hiding her from me, and I highly doubt he's doing it. You and Cassidy became friends. I need to know where she is. She needs to come home."

"You need? What about what she needs? Why not leave her alone, Sean? Cassidy has made the decision that will allow her to move on and have a life—a family. She's done chasing a man who doesn't love or want her. She's safe, I promise you. Just leave her alone. Let her find happiness and love."

My fist came down hard on the table. I leaned toward her, letting Everly see how angry and desperate I was. Smoke gave me a quelling look.

"Don't. I'm hanging on by a thread, Everly. I have to see her and talk to her. I can't wait. Please, this is killing me."

"What is? You not being able to fulfill the role of a big brother? She still has two of those. She can survive without a third. We all thought you would admit to feeling more than that for her after that mission, but we were wrong. Getting away to start a new life is exactly what she needs," Everly added.

"Not without me! Goddamn it. If you want me to beg, then I will. Please tell me where she is. I can't go on like this. It has nothing to do with being her big brother.

I'm done denying it. I love her. I want to spend my life with her. I can't do that if she won't talk to me. Tell me where she is," I begged.

She didn't say anything. She just studied me. Smoke glanced from her to me and back. "Tigress, is there something you want to tell me?"

"Maybe. I helped Cassidy leave Virginia. She wanted to start over but couldn't do it when she always had to see him. Cassidy isn't able to give other men a chance because of him. The way I hear it, she's dating someone. I guess the distance was the answer. I don't want to ruin it for her."

A pain shot through my chest, hearing Cassidy was dating. On the heels of it came fury and resolve. There was no goddamn way she fell out of love with me in a month. She might be seeing someone, but she didn't love him.

"What do you want me to do to prove I'm ready to commit to her fully? I need to tell her how much I fucking love her and want to marry her. I want her to be the mother of my children and no one else."

"Do you think she'll believe it? You've denied it for years, and now you suddenly want to declare it after she moves away. It sounds suspicious to me, and it will to her. How about all those women you dated and fucked that she had to see you with? Do you think she can easily forget those? You threw Josie in her face not long ago, right here."

"No, I don't think she'll forget them or the idiot I was. I know I hurt her. I'll spend the rest of my life making up for it. I only did it to try to forget her, but it never worked. As for Josie, I was pretending. I never touched her or anyone else when we were here. Unlike me having to watch her with Falcon and then knowing I drove her to sleep with him. I have to live with the fact my woman has been with other men because of my stupidity. I let my promise to Mark and my concern that he would object to us being together overrule my heart. I'm done. I need to know where she is. I'll grovel until she forgives me and agrees she'll be mine."

"What if she refuses?" she shot back.

"Then I'll hold out hope until the day she marries someone else. Then I'll end my misery."

"End it? How?" Smoke asked.

"How would you end it if Everly was forever denied to you?" I asked him grimly.

I stood there as the two of them exchanged looks. Finally, Smoke spoke. "Ev, tell him. They need to hash this out. They have to take talk even if there's only a slim chance they can make this right."

She nibbled on her lower lip, then answered him, though she stared at me. "I can't tell him where she is, but if someone else were to tell him, then I haven't gone back on my promise. She's my friend. Smoke, she's at the place where I used to live. I offered it to her while she was here."

A smile spread across his face. "Come with me, and I'll get you the address. Don't make us regret this, Sean." He gestured for me to follow him. As I walked past her, I paused and kissed Everly on the cheek. She smacked mine.

"Don't make me regret this. If you do, I'll erase your whole existence," she warned me.

"I won't. I promise."

Excitement bubbled up inside of me. By this time tomorrow, I'd be with Cassidy, working my hardest to get her to be mine. All I needed was a little luck and a whole lot of forgiveness. No matter what she demanded of me, I'd do it, as long as it wasn't leaving her.

෴

I was too impatient to drive from Tennessee to Florida, even though it was shorter than the drive from Virginia. I knew I'd probably kill myself speeding. Instead, I stayed overnight at the compound since it was late when I got there. The following morning, I boarded a flight to Florida. Smoke and Everly let me stay the night with them. I went to the clubhouse, said hi to the others, and spent a little time chatting with them, but kept the reason I was there under wraps. I brushed it off as I was passing through for the night.

I could barely keep myself in control to sit still on the plane or prevent myself from shoving people out of the way to run off the plane to get to the car rental place when we landed. I sped off as soon as I had my car, and the address to Everly's house entered into the GPS device. It was Saturday morning. I was hoping she was still at home and not out. There was a chance she could be. Cassidy was an early riser and didn't believe in lazing about, even if it was her day off. If she weren't there, I'd have to call and see if Everly could track her. I wouldn't be able to wait for her to come back.

I'd talked to Smoke and Everly about Cassidy, the move, and my feelings for her. Ev was an excellent friend and didn't reveal anything specific that might've been said other than the fact Cassidy was seeing someone. I knew that was deliberate. She wanted me to hurt, and I deserved it.

Pulling up to the address forty minutes later, I examined the neighborhood. Everly had a lovely house in what appeared to be a great neighborhood. There were a few people out mowing grass or puttering in their yards. Down here, everything was green and in bloom, as if it were the middle of summer. Back home, we just looked like spring had barely hit. Seeing the towering palm trees was weird, but it was also cool. The only tropical places I ever went to weren't those you went to sightsee. And those were few and far between. Most had been to the deserts of the world.

I parked on the street outside the house. Her car was in the driveway. I sat there a couple of moments to settle my racing heart, then I got out and went to the door. I knocked firmly. Slender windows on either side of it allowed you to peek out but not gain access. I saw movement. My eyes zeroed in on the figure approaching the door. Cassidy's face showed astonishment, quickly replaced with panic, and then it was wiped smooth. She stared back at me through the panes of glass without opening the door.

"Cassidy, let me in. We need to talk, and I won't leave until we do," I called through the door.

"You will if I call the cops and have you arrested for trespassing," she shouted back.

"Since you're not the owner, you might have difficulty getting that to stick. And even if you do, we have lawyers and contacts who can get me out within the hour. Do you really wanna play this game or be an adult and face me?" I knew accusing her of being childish would piss her off, and she'd have to open the door. She hated nothing more than to be called less than an adult.

She moved, and then the door flew open. She was ticked. "How dare you call me childish, you egotistical bastard! Not wanting to see or speak to you doesn't make me a child!" she snapped.

Before she had a chance to slam the door on me, I pushed inside, backing her up far enough to shut it behind me. Realizing what I'd done, she moved to put distance between us. She took up a defensive position.

"Cass, you don't need to be afraid. I'm not here to hurt you."

She snorted. I swore she muttered, "Since when." I winced. I deserved that. She was right. I might not have hurt her physically, but I'd done it over and over emotionally.

"Please, can we sit and talk? There are so many things we need to discuss."

Instead of answering me, she walked off. I followed and ended up in a sunroom at the back of the house. She took a seat in a chair, so I had no choice but to sit on a loveseat across from her but not too close.

We sat there for a minute, just studying each other. This was going badly, not that I had anyone to blame but myself. I think a tiny part of me hoped she'd see me and realize she didn't hate me, and she'd throw herself in my arms and declare she was mine. Yeah, I was an idiot. Finally, she spoke.

"You have five minutes. Say what you came here to say, then leave."

"Five minutes isn't enough time."

"It's all the time you're getting. How did you find me?"

"That's not important. What is is us. I know I've hurt you, and you've had enough. I don't blame you for leaving, but you have to hear me out."

"Sean, my days of listening to you and doing as you say are over. What about this, don't you get? I've finally grown up and moved on to have a life. I'm happy here. I have a job, and I'm making friends. You no longer have to be my big brother. I can take care of myself."

"I'm not your goddamn brother! And I heard about the friends you're making. Who is the guy you're dating?" I snapped.

A flash of surprise changed to a smirk. "Who I'm dating is none of your business. Is that why you came here? To lecture me on what I can and can't do? Because if it is, that boat sailed a long time ago. I'll tell you like I told you in Dublin Falls. Who I choose to fuck or spend time with is none of your business."

Anger was bubbling inside of me at the thought of her sleeping with this unknown guy. Had she done it to spite me, even if I never found out? I thought she had a thing for Falcon, but maybe she didn't. Her sudden behavior of being intimate with multiple men wasn't like her. Had I driven her to this? Images of her with a faceless man in bed flashed in my head, and all thoughts of talking calmly and logically went out the window. I came bounding to my feet. I stopped myself from snatching her up and kissing her by pacing. I had to clench my fists to keep my hands off her.

"What the hell has gotten into you!? You've never been someone who jumps from man to man. You date guys but not one right after another, and you certainly don't hop from one man's bed to the next."

"You mean, since when did I become like you? Well, see, I realized something. I've been a blind fool who kept wishing for something that would never happen. Congratulations, you finally made me see the truth. I should thank you, to be honest. I'm now free to do anything I want. No more waiting on someone else to make me happy. That's my job. I thought I'd see what the attraction has been for you all these years. I mean, who knows, I may settle down one day, or I might not, but if I do, I know I won't be a disappointment to my partner in the sack. I have a lot of time to make up for." She smirked as she said it.

I saw red. Letting out a roar, I lunged at her. She tried to get out of the chair but wasn't fast enough. I pinned her there. Her eyes were wide. I didn't think. I just acted. I slammed my mouth down on hers. I trapped her head with my hands in her hair, and the way I pinned her body with mine, there was no way for her to get away or effectively fight me. She had skills, and I wasn't stupid enough to let her use them on me.

She tried to tear her mouth away, but I held her still. I nibbled and pressed my lips to hers to evoke a response. She refused to respond. Pressing closer, I slipped out my tongue to tease her lips. I wanted her to open. I needed to taste her. I'd been dreaming of kissing her and what she'd taste like for years. I was done waiting. She squirmed and tried to get leverage to shove me away, but I was too big and too skilled for her to do it. I began pressing tiny kisses all over her mouth. As I did, I whispered to her.

"Baby, please, open up. I need to taste you."

She made protesting noises, but that was it. As time ticked by without her responding, desperation filled me. What if she genuinely didn't love me anymore? Had I been successful in killing her love? As this harsh possibility settled over me, tears pricked my eyes, and desolation filled me. I eased back and kneeled there with my head hanging. She didn't say anything for several heartbeats.

"Sean?" she queried hesitantly.

I stood up. I didn't make eye contact with her. I couldn't. I was trying not to cry like a baby. "Cassidy, don't change who you are. Don't become like me and be a coward. You're perfect the way you've always been. I'm sorry. I shouldn't have come here. I hope the next man you love knows how lucky he is and deserves you. I know it's too late to say this, but I do love you and have loved you for a long time. I'm sorry I killed your love for me. Know that I'll go to my grave loving you. No worries, I won't bother you again."

Unable to stand anymore, I whirled around and headed for the front door. I heard her moving behind me, but I ignored her. I had to get out of here. My mind was a chaotic mess. I opened the door and stepped outside when her hands closed around my arm.

"Sean, stop. Look at me."

"I can't. Goodbye," I said, yanking my arm loose and hurried to my car. She was shouting my name. I saw her coming after me, but I didn't stop. I jumped inside, closed the door, and had the engine on before she got to me. She pounded on the window. I saw fear on her face. I mouthed *I love you* then took off.

I didn't know where I was going, and I didn't care. My thoughts were scattered. A thousand things were going through my mind at once, but the one that kept repeating was I'd never have her, and it was all my fault. We could've been together for the past seven years if I hadn't been a coward. I should've claimed her the moment she turned eighteen. We could've had a family by now. Instead, I kept being stupid and refused to face the real reason I never told her I loved her. It had nothing to do with Mark and him being upset at me.

I was so caught up in my misery that I didn't see the truck run the red light until it was too late. I saw it seconds before it plowed into me. Agonizing pain shot through me as I hit the steering wheel, the airbag deployed, and I was slammed back into the seat. Pain was radiating throughout my body. My head was fuzzy, and things were going dark. I swear, right before I blacked out, I heard Cassidy's voice calling my name. I smiled. At least she'd be with me at the end.

Cassidy:

My head was whirling as I followed Sean. His unexpected visit had thrown me, and I didn't know what to say or do. I automatically wanted to hurt him when he asked about the man I was dating. My shot about becoming like him was a lie. There was no way I'd ever be able to jump from man to man. The truth was, I was scared.

The instant I saw him, I felt my resolve begin to waver and rapidly leak away. When he kissed me, it was all I could do not to respond. I was about to break when he moved away. The things he said scared me. I didn't like the tone of his voice. He sounded dead. I knew I had to follow him when he rushed out of the house and got into his car. Luckily, I'd been about to leave the house when he showed up, so my keys, ID, and bank card were in my pocket. I hated to carry a purse. I ran to my car and took off after him.

He drove aimlessly, but despite that, he wasn't reckless. Sean was too controlled and careful to put others in danger. Even when he went faster than he should, he was cautious. I had no clue if he had a destination in mind. I didn't know the area well enough yet to know where he might be headed.

I was a couple of cars behind him when a large delivery truck ran the red light and plowed into him. I screamed and watched in horror as his car spun around in the middle of the intersection. I don't know how the others with the right of way like us kept from hitting him or anyone else. The driver of the truck that hit him kept going.

I somehow pulled my car off to the side of the road and got out. Heedless of the danger, I ran to his car. Despite being terrified, I had enough sense to yell at those getting out of their cars to call 911. I kicked into training mode. The guys, Mark and Dad, had not only trained me in all manner of self-defense and weapons but also made sure I had what they called combat medic training. As SEALs, they all had it.

Getting to the driver's door, I saw him slumped over the deflating airbag. There was blood on it and his face. His eyes were closed, and he wasn't moving or making a sound. The glass had shattered out of the driver's window. Reaching my shaking hands inside, I felt for his pulse. I was terrified it wouldn't be there. It took a few moments for it to register that it was. When it did, I sagged in relief.

"Sean, can you hear me? It's Cassie. Open your eyes. I need to know how badly you're hurt, my love," I asked hoarsely, trying not to cry. He didn't respond. Grabbing the door handle, I attempted to yank it open, but it was crushed, so I only got it partially open. I growled in frustration and jerked harder.

"Here, let me help with that," a man said from behind me, making me jump. Glancing back, I nodded. I needed to get closer so I could assess Sean. I yanked on the door handle while the stranger pulled on the door frame. I noted he had on gloves, which protected his hands from the shards of glass. That's when it registered that he was dressed as a biker. Opening the door far enough for me to squeeze inside took a few tries.

"What else can I do?" the biker asked.

"See that white car over there?" I pointed to mine. He nodded. "There's a first aid bag in the backseat. Will you get it for me, please?"

"Sure will," he said before jogging off. I gave my attention to Sean.

I rechecked his pulse, then lightly tapped his cheek. "Sean, open your eyes." When it didn't work, I called louder and used his team name. "Fiend! Attention, sailor!"

That got a slight twitch out of him. Before I could repeat it, the man was back. I took the open bag. Finding gauze, I tore it open with my teeth and wadded it up to press to the head wound that was bleeding everywhere.

"Here, let me hold that," the biker said.

I didn't bother to argue. I let him do it so I could check Sean's pupils and call his name more. I heard people talking and shouting, but I ignored them. The wail of sirens was in the background. I hoped it was the paramedics and not just cops coming to the scene.

"Fiend, talk to me! It's Cassidy," I growled.

Sean groaned, but he didn't open his eyes.

"Fiend, is he a biker?" my helper asked.

"No, although we know a bunch. He was a Navy SEAL. It was his team name."

"Ah, got it. I served with a bunch of SEALs. My name is Vader."

"Thank you for helping, Vader."

"You're welcome. I saw what happened. That truck just kept going. I got a partial plate."

"I'll need that." I was busy trying to assess Sean and talk while fighting my panic.

"Sir, ma'am, please move back. We've got this,"

another man's voice startled me. Looking over my shoulder, I saw a fireman standing there. He was carrying a bag, which told me he was a paramedic. Reluctantly, I moved back along with Vader. I was so into Sean that I hadn't noticed the firemen and police arriving.

Police were being mobbed by people trying to tell them what happened. I stood there watching the only person who mattered. Suddenly, I was snapped into action. I fumbled to get my phone out of my back pocket. When I had it, I dialed the first number in my most frequently dialed. Gabe picked up.

"Hey Cass, this is a surprise. How're you?"

"Gabe, I need your help. Sean came to see me. He's been in an accident. A truck hit his car, then fled. We're at the intersection of Graves and Hunt in Jacksonville, Florida. Vader, tell my friend the partial license number and anything else you know about the truck. We need to get working on finding whoever that bastard was. He didn't even bother to stop."

Gabe started swearing. Vader gave me an odd look, but he did as I asked. He had the truck's color, model, and half the license plate. When he was done, I went back to talking to Gabe.

"How long ago did this happen?" he asked.

"About ten minutes maybe, I don't know. Gabe, he's not responsive. He's bleeding from his head. I don't know how badly he's hurt. What if he dies?" I sobbed.

"He's not going to die. If he does, I'll go to hell and bring his ass back and then kick it for doing it. He's a tough bastard. Many have tried to kill Fiend and have failed. Find out where they plan to take him."

"They'll take him to UFHealth. It's the closest," Vader informed me.

"UF?"

"Ahh, yeah, the University of Florida Health is a Trauma One center. He'll be in great hands."

"Thank you."

"I got it. You get your ass to the hospital. We'll be there as fast as we can. Gonna get the bird in the air. You stay with him," Gabe ordered.

"I will," was all I could choke out. Gabe said a few other things, but I couldn't focus. All I could do was stare at the fireman working to get Sean out of the car. If he died, I wouldn't be able to go on.

Cassidy: Chapter 6

The trip to the hospital was a jumbled mess. The cops tried to make me stay at the scene, but somehow, Vader came to the rescue and got them to let me go. I gave them my information and assured them I'd be at the hospital. It wasn't like they didn't have enough witnesses clamoring to tell them what happened. They could wait to get my statement.

When I pulled into the hospital's parking lot, I was oddly relieved to see Vader park next to me. I'd been so preoccupied that I hadn't noticed him following me, which was stupid. I should always be aware of my surroundings. The guys would chew me out if they knew I hadn't been.

He led me inside and to the ER. It was clear he'd been here before by how he navigated without looking at the signs. He escorted me to the registration window. I had to fight my anger at the woman's insistence I fill out a crapload of forms to register Sean. I wanted to be with him and know what was happening. If it wasn't for Vader, I don't know what I would've done. I probably would've punched her in the face, which wasn't fair to her. The woman was doing her job.

Time dragged by for me. After filling out all the information, which, thankfully, I knew, I paced. They were working on him and wouldn't let me in the back. For some reason, Vader stuck with me. I lost track of time.

The cops eventually appeared and asked me questions. I answered the best I could, but it didn't seem to be good enough. They seemed to be trying to pin the blame for the accident on Sean.

I was about to tell them if they asked me the same thing one more time, they could go fuck themselves when the door to the ER opened, and in rushed two sights for sore eyes. I left the one officer mid-sentence and ran to them. Griffin was the one to grab me first and hug me. He squeezed me tightly, and then, after placing a kiss on my cheek, he passed me off to Gabe to get the same treatment from him. I breathed easier just having them here, my brothers. When they let go, I heard a throat clear behind me. Turning, I faced the cop I'd left, O'Grady. He wasn't looking pleased. His partner was with him. He was quieter but no less judgmental, in my opinion. A couple of feet behind them was Vader.

"Ms. O'Rourke, we're super busy. We need to finish our conversation. Who are these gentlemen?" O'Grady asked.

"Officer, I have answered the same questions for you three times. My answer isn't changing. I'm done. If you come up with new ones, you can call me. You have my contact information. I need to concentrate on Sean. I have people I need to bring up to date and keep informed."

"And what's your involvement in this?" O'Grady asked Gabe and Griff.

Before either could answer, I did. "Who they are is none of your business? Do you treat all victims and their families like this? You act as if we did something wrong. People at the scene told you how the other guy ran the light. You have CCTV cameras. Check them out. They'll show we're telling the truth. I have no idea who was driving the truck, nor do I know of any reason someone would have to target Sean. I told you, and so did Vader, that the other driver ran the light," I pointed to the silent biker. "Sean wasn't drinking, nor does he use drugs. You're now pushing to the harassment stage."

"I'd be careful using the word harassment. Your acquaintance here isn't exactly reliable. How do we know this isn't some insurance scheme you're pulling?" his partner, Tavern, asked.

My outrage was tempered by Gabe and Griff coming to life. Gabe took out his phone and dialed a number. I had no idea who he was calling, but moments later, I smiled.

"I need you to find us the name and number of the police chief here in Jacksonville. Let him or her know we need to file a complaint about Officers O'Grady and Tavern. They're harassing Cassidy and us at the hospital, making unfounded allegations. Also, call Flanagan and have him get here as soon as possible. As of this moment, all questions will go through him. Call me as soon as you have everything done." He paused to listen for about a minute, then continued. "I don't know. The cops are preventing us from finding out how Sean is, but as soon as I know, I'll let you know. Thanks, Margie," he said before he hung up. I fought not to stick my tongue out at the two cops. They were pissed.

"Our lawyer is on his way. He'll be coming from Virginia, but they'll fly him down, so it shouldn't take more than a couple of hours to get him here, just like it did for us. He'll be representing you if you like, Vader. No more answers until then. Officers, Ms. O'Rourke, and the three of us are done talking. Excuse us. Our brother needs our attention," Gabe told them before walking past them. I followed him. Vader dropped in beside me, and Griff brought up the back. The cops stood there stunned. If they hadn't been assholes, it would've never gotten to this point.

"I like your friends," Vader whispered to me.

I laughed. "Me too."

From that moment on, things began to move. Griff went to speak to the lady at the check-in window. It wasn't long before a doctor came out to talk to us. Within twenty minutes at the most, we had an update, and I was shown into the back to sit with Sean. The guys were just as anxious to be with him but insisted it was my place. They knew how much I loved him. They remained in the waiting room talking to Vader.

When I reached his bedside, I couldn't help it. I laid my head next to his on the pillow and wept as I whispered to him. "Sean, God, I can't lose you. I love you. I'm sorry I lied to you. I'm not seriously dating anyone or sleeping with countless men. I went out twice, but there was nothing there. I left home because being near you and not being with you was killing me. I'll always love you. You're my heart and soul. Please, come back to us. I promise I'll come home if you do. I won't hold you to what you said at the house. I know you were just trying to get me to come back, but I don't care."

Something grazing my cheek made my eyes open. It was Sean's hand. I gasped and raised my head to find his eyes open, and he was staring at me. His gaze was intense for someone who'd just woken up. I gulped. Was he cognizant? Had he heard what I said? Would he forgive me for pushing him to take off? It was my fault he was in this hospital bed. I went to stand up, but his hand grasped my chin and held me there.

"Sean, do you know who I am?" I asked hesitantly.

"I do," he said somewhat hoarsely.

"Do you remember what happened?"

"Yes. I was driving, and a truck ran a red light and hit my car."

"Yes, it did. Oh God, I'm sorry. It's all my fault," I admitted as tears began to fall. I tried to move away again, but his other hand came up and hooked behind my neck.

"It's not your fault."

"Yes, it is. I drove you to take off. You were upset. If you hadn't been, you would've seen that truck sooner and been able to avoid it." I told him. He tried to sit up. "Stop moving! They're still running tests. I need to tell someone you're awake. Stay still," I commanded before attempting to move again.

He held me still. The next thing I knew, he was pulling my head down, and right before our lips met, he whispered, "I meant every word I said. I love you, Cassidy. If you want me to be alright, then you tell me what I have to do to earn your forgiveness," he uttered before kissing me. Unlike the kiss at the house, I responded to this one. I kissed him back eagerly and passionately, the same way he was kissing me.

Sean:

Coming awake from being unconscious, it took a few seconds for me to realize that was what was happening, and finding the woman I love crying next to me and promising she'd come back and not hold me to my words of love was enough to snap me entirely out of the haze. There was no way I'd let her back out. I heard her say she loved me. Touching her face and having her react with tears had me trying to assure her that the accident wasn't her fault. It was that asshole driving the truck. When she continued to say it was her fault, I pushed to drive home that I meant every word I said about loving her and asking her how to get her forgiveness.

The tears and her beloved face were too much. I knew the last kiss failed epically, but I had to kiss her again. When she responded, I let the bliss of it take over. There was passion behind her kiss, just like there was in mine. This time, when I teased her lips with the tip of my tongue, she immediately opened and let me slip my tongue inside. Her tongue came to meet mine, and it twined around it.

For years, I'd tried to imagine what it would be like to kiss her and what she'd taste like. My imagination didn't come close to how wonderful reality was. Cassidy always had this thing for Jolly Ranchers candy. She loved them, no matter the flavor. She had since she was a kid. We loved to tease her about it, and we'd leave gifts of them randomly for her. You'd think we left her diamonds when she'd get them.

It should've been no surprise that she tasted sweet like them, but underneath the sweet candy taste was a different sweet—one that I could only think was her. I avidly deepened the kiss, but I couldn't seem to get enough. I tried to bring her closer. As I did, I became aware I was getting hard. Hell, I was always half-hard whenever I was around her, even having an innocent conversation. It was no shock to find myself fully there when we kissed. She moved closer and pressed her body to mine. When she did, I became aware of other sensations. These weren't so welcome. It was pain and soreness. I hissed. That broke the spell, and she was pulling away from me in a blink.

Her face was flushed, and she was breathing a little hard, which I loved to see, but I saw worry and remorse on her face, too. "Shit, I'm sorry. I didn't mean to hurt you," she exclaimed. She tried to move away from the bed, but I grabbed her hand to keep her there. I wanted the least distance between us possible.

"Don't move. I know you didn't. It's just a few sore spots. More kisses will make it all better," I said with a smile.

That got her frown to change to a smile. "I bet they would, but you need to see the doctor. I need to get someone."

"Then go get someone, but please, don't leave. Come back."

Her tender look made me relax. "No one is getting rid of me. I'll be right back. Try to relax. Tension will only make the pain worse."

I reluctantly let go of her. If she slipped away, I'd

get out of this bed no matter how much it hurt and hunt her down. I wasn't losing her again. Now that she confessed she still loved me, nothing would stop me from convincing her that I loved her and that we were meant to be together. I was a man with a mission, and they didn't call me Fiend for no reason.

Most people would take the name to mean I was evil, a devil. In my case, it referred to a lesser-known definition of the word. Fiend meant expert, too. With things that I found worth it, I became highly knowledgeable and skilled in them. I relentlessly pursued and perfected the knowledge and skills pertaining to them. The guys in my SEAL team who gave me the name said I would lock on and never stop until satisfied. Acquiring Cassidy and her love would be my most fiendish effort. I would excel at being a lover and partner to her in every way.

As I waited impatiently and somewhat anxiously for her to return, I recalled the accident, the impact moment, and the subsequent pain, more specifically. Damn, that had hurt. It wasn't the worst pain I'd ever felt, but the residual was making itself known. My head was pounding, and my upper chest felt like every bone had been broken. It was funny that I felt none of it when I was kissing her. As time ticked by, I grew more anxious. Goddamn it, she'd left. When the curtain opened, I was trying to sit up and get the rail down on the bed. In stepped a man and a woman. Relief filled me as they parted to go to either side of my bed. There was Cassidy. Her smile changed to a frown.

"Sean, what in the world are you doing?" she asked. Her hands went to her hips, and she crooked an eyebrow at me. I loved that look, even when it was aimed at me.

I gave her my best innocent look. "Nothing."

"Bullshit. You were trying to get up. Are you trying to make your injuries worse? I swear, if you don't stay there and let them make sure you're alright, I'll tie you to that bed."

I couldn't help it. The words slipped out. "Baby, if you want to tie me up, all you gotta do is say so. Though I'd prefer if it were somewhere more private."

She blushed. The doctor chuckled softly, and the nurse giggled. Doc was the one to come to the rescue. "Well, I see you're alert and able to converse. I'd like to check out a few other things, Mr. Walterson, to be sure of the full extent of your injuries. I do ask that you wait on the tying up, though." He grinned as he said it. I liked him already.

Cassidy groaned and covered her face with her hand. "He won't die if he can say stuff like that. Why don't you do whatever you need to do? I need to go to the waiting area."

"Cass, please, don't leave. I'll behave," I said hastily.

She came to stand next to the nurse and took my hand. She squeezed it. "Sean, I'm not leaving-leaving. I'll come back as soon as they're done. I need to tell Griff and Gabe that you're awake and talking. They're worried to death but allowed me to sit with you. I'm not leaving the hospital. I promise on Mark's soul."

Hearing her say Mark's name made me want to cringe, but I didn't. That was another sin I'd have to make up for one day, God willing. She had no idea the secret the three of us kept about her brother. Hopefully, she'd be too happy to hate us for keeping her in the dark when she found out.

"They're here?"

"Of course they are. Surely you didn't think I wouldn't call them or they wouldn't come running? They flew in. Now, let them do what they need to do. I'll be back as soon as I can," she said before dropping a swift kiss on my mouth, and then she was gone.

"Alright, let's get started. I'm Dr. Troy, and this is Nurse Pia. You're a fortunate man. So far, our tests show a better scenario than we hoped for. While you were out, we did an MRI. You appear not to have any internal injuries to major organs or bleeding that we can see. The organs in your upper body have been bruised. Your sternum and ribs, while painful, I have no doubt, aren't fractured by some miracle. You have hard bones."

"What about my head? It hurts like hell," I asked.

"Ah, yes, we didn't see anything on the brain MRI other than a concussion, but we'd like to be sure. We want you to stay here a while to ensure nothing unexpected crops up. Before you leave, we'll do another set of MRIs to be sure. You did strike your head hard, and there's a laceration there in addition to the concussion. Also, we did have to do bloodwork. The police insisted we test you for the presence of drugs and alcohol. We did it because they had a warrant. I've never seen them get one that fast. I thought you should know."

"Alcohol and drugs, why the hell would they need that? I was the victim of the accident. I guess I can see how they have to rule out everything, but—" I was cut off by the curtain opening again. Only this time, it wasn't Cassidy or even my brothers. It was two men in uniform, cops. As they entered my space without asking, Cassidy, Gabe, and Griff came right behind them. Those three were glaring at the back of the cops' heads.

"Officers, you can't be in here yet. I'm not done

assessing Mr. Walterson," Dr. Troy reprimanded them.

"We have some questions for him. He seems wide awake to me. What were the results of his toxicology tests?" the taller cop asked.

Before the doctor could answer, Gabe pushed forward and crowded the cops. He was giving them his best pissed-off look. You didn't mess with Midas unless you wanted him to fuck up your life or take it.

"Officer O'Grady, you and your partner were informed that no questions would be answered until our lawyer arrived. You lost that privilege when you badgered Cassidy and Vader. You seem more worried about finding some way to pin the accident on our brother than the man who ran the red light. We'd like to know why. I have your chief's name and number. Should I call him? As for toxicology results, those will be shared if our lawyer deems you've gone through the proper channels to have them drawn. Sean, good to see you awake, brother. Say nothing."

I smiled and relaxed back. Usually, I'd take the lead and lay down the law to someone like this, but I was content to let Gabe and Griffin do it this time. O'Grady's scowl grew darker. His partner was casting angry looks at my brothers and Cassidy. I didn't like it. I held out my hand.

"Cassie, baby, come here. I need your hand." I might've phrased it more as an order than a request, but she skirted around the cops and came right to me. She smiled and took my hand.

"Listen, I don't know what your people's problem is, but we have a job—," the other cop said but was cut off by Dr. Troy.

"This is a hospital. You can't be back here. Officers,

please go back to the waiting area. It seems you have to wait for a lawyer. As for the three of you, I'll give you a couple of minutes to say hi, and then all but one of you has to leave. I promise we'll get him situated as fast as we can."

Boring holes through us, if possible, the officers reluctantly left. When they did, all of us relaxed. Doc rolled his eyes. "I don't know what's got into those two. We've dealt with them before, but I've not seen them this insistent."

"I have. Sometimes, they seem to get an idea in their heads, and they want to badger certain people," Pia stated softly.

"Flanagan will take care of them. He should be here soon. So, how's he doing, Doc? Sorry, how rude of me. I'm Gabriel Pagett, and this is Griffin Voss. We're this one's best friends." He held his hand out to the doctor. They shook hands, and then Griffin shook the doc's. They nodded to the nurse since she was on the opposite side of the bed.

"Gentlemen, nice to meet you. I'm Dr. Troy, and this is Pia. Are you alright with me sharing your medical condition with these three? I've got to ask."

"They're the only three who have permission to know everything or to make decisions for me. Make sure that's noted on my chart."

"Pia, make sure to do that. Let me review what we already told Mr. Walterson, and then we can go from there. I still need to do a physical exam."

"Call me Sean, please."

He nodded and then got to talking. He didn't share anything new. When he was done, my crew asked him how long I might be here, and they all gave me awkward hugs because I was in bed. They promised to be back soon, then left. Cassidy remained behind.

"Miss, I'm going to do a physical exam. Are you staying…" Dr. Troy petered off.

"I'll step outside the curtain. I'll be back as soon as they're done, Sean."

As much as I didn't care what she saw, I didn't want her to be uncomfortable. Maybe being banged up wasn't the image I wanted in her head. I let her go. Troy and Pia got to it after she was on the other side of the curtain. He rattled off things to her, mainly orders, and she assisted when he wanted to do things like roll me over to check out my backside. I admit, being in this gown and having a woman who I wasn't planning to have sex with see my cock and ass was rather weird. Especially when Cassidy was outside the curtain. As odd as it sounded, I felt like I was cheating on her. Eventually, they finished up, and Cass was called back inside. She came right to my side and held my hand.

"Well, you're lucky. There are a few small nicks and lacerations from the flying glass—nothing serious or needing sutures. The cut on your head will need to be kept clean and dry. We'll go over how to care for it later. Movement will be painful for a while. We'd like to keep you for observation for the next few hours. We'll move you to a different area for that. As long as you exhibit no new issues, you should be able to go home later today. I'll say it again: you were fortunate. We'll get you moved over. You can have two visitors at a time there."

Wanting to do whatever it took to get out of here, I didn't disagree. As Dr. Troy and Pia got things in place to move me, I stayed there, content to hold Cassie's hand. I knew we needed to talk, but not here. I'd wait until we got out of here.

Cassidy: Chapter 7 - Current Day

My napping was at an end. I'd been lost in memories of Sean and me and how we'd gotten to this point. I guess overall, they'd been happy ones, although we did have our moments. Complicated described us. Jumping as another contraction hit me, I tried to move in the bed. My eyes opened. Sean was standing over me with a concerned look.

"Foxy, what can I do for you? Are you in pain? I thought the epidural was supposed to stop that."

"It's not painful, just more pressure. The contractions are getting more intense and closer together. It means we're closer to meeting our son."

Ignoring hospital rules, he lowered the bedrail and gently moved me over to make as much room as possible for himself. He had to lay on his side, but he did it. I snuggled into his chest. I always felt better when he was near and could hold me, and I could inhale his scent.

His hands began to rub my back and side. He kissed me, and it was a long and sweet one. When he stopped, I wanted to beg him to continue, but he had something to say. "I can't believe we're here. It's been over four years since we finally got our shit together. I've loved every damn day of it, but having Noah and now Nash, I can't tell you how it makes me feel. I never knew I could love anyone until I met Mark, Griffin, and Gabe. Then we came home, and I discovered you and Adam and then Jessie and

Graden. I thought I'd won the lottery when I never truly had anyone love me. It was too much to expect anyone to love me the way you did and do. Now, to have you and the kids to love and have you love me back. It's a goddamn gift beyond any gift."

I knew his past and why he'd been so stubborn about admitting he loved me. We'd worked that out years ago, but he was still, at times, haunted by it. He got moments of worry that he didn't deserve us or that he'd lose us. I found I had to help him through those. He never saw himself as a gift, which he was to me.

"Honey, we're all blessed. I feel the same way about you and the kids. I can't think of what I did to deserve you and them. And to have Gabe and Griffin. And don't get me started on having Mark back. Then, they added Sloan, Gemma, and Hadley to the mix. I have sisters! And a niece and nephew with another coming. My life is so blessed, but it wouldn't be half as wonderful if it weren't for you, Noah, and Nash. I love you, Sean Walterson, more every day."

His mouth crashing down on mine was his answer to my declaration. He kissed me passionately. So much so that even though I was in labor, I responded. My nipples hardened, and I was sure my pussy got slick. The man could probably turn me on in the middle of a gunfight. He was potent, to say the least. When he finally let go of me, I was panting. He smirked. I smacked my hand onto his chest.

"Bastard, you did that on purpose."

"Hey, I can't help if you took it that way. And you're not innocent. See." His hand captured mine. It was brought between us, so I could feel his erection straining against his zipper. To pay him back, I squeezed then rubbed up and down his bulge.

He growled in warning. "If you don't stop, the nurses and Doc Maggio will come in and find my cock in that sexy mouth."

I knew he was teasing me, but the thought made me hotter. "Baby, I'll suck your cock anytime, anyplace. If you can make it so I can reach you, I'm game," I taunted as I rubbed his erection harder.

He groaned louder and closed his eyes. I kept going, and I was wondering if I would get him off in his jeans when there was a knock on the door. He yanked the sheet up over us and hoarsely yelled, "Come in."

The door opened, and in came Mark and Sloan. My brother walked to the bed. He shook his head. "If you two are carrying on, stop it. Christ, she hasn't even had the second one, and you're trying to get her pregnant again?"

The old me would've been mortified that my brother knew I'd been fooling around. Sean had cured me of that. He didn't believe in hiding our feelings. He kept us from being arrested, but that was it. Sloan was reprimanding Mark.

"Stop it! As if you're any better."

He smiled at her, tenderly placing his hand on her flat stomach and rubbing back and forth. "What can I say? You're fucking irresistible, and I'm potent."

As his words sank in, I gasped and tried to wiggle to face them better. Sean shifted me. "Potent? Are you telling us something, brother?" I asked excitedly.

Sloan sighed. "We were waiting until I was twelve weeks to say anything. Plus, we didn't want to steal the spotlight from you two or Griff and Hadley. Their baby is due before ours."

I clapped my hands and squealed for joy. Sloan

smiled, and Mark smirked. "When are you due?" I asked.

"March twenty-third, six weeks after Hadley. I knew he couldn't keep quiet much longer. The man can't keep a secret," she joked.

"Hey, I keep secrets better than anyone," he protested, and what he said was the truth. He'd kept the fact he wasn't dead and his real identity a secret for five years.

"Don't remind us. Did you just come in to check on us, or was there something else?" I asked.

"Well, it wasn't to see you two getting it on. We wanted to see how it was going. We have an anxious crew waiting to meet this little guy. Can you hurry it up, sis?" Mark added with a wink.

"Oh sure, let me adhere to your schedule! God, he thinks he can make anyone adhere to his wants and needs," I huffed, although I wasn't truly upset.

"Damn right. If people would listen, things would go much smoother. Listen here, Nash, this is your Uncle Mark. We want to meet you, so get a move on. There's a whole shitload of spoiling waiting out here. And before you know it, you'll be out shooting and having all sorts of other fun with me, Uncle Griff, Uncle Gabe, and your dad. We have plans." he directed to my stomach.

Sloan and I met each other's eyes and rolled them. There was no way to counter that, so we didn't even try. His remarks got Sean and Mark talking about future trips they planned to take the boys on. Sloan interrupted them.

"Whoa, wait a minute. Don't think for an instant Greer and or any other daughters we have are to be excluded. I'd think with me and Cassidy here, you'd know that wasn't happening. And I wouldn't let Gemma or Hadley hear you talk like this. Our girls will be as trained to protect themselves and others as our boys."

"Slo, no one is excluding our daughters," Mark assured her as she gave him a narrow-eyed look.

"Babe, our girls will be doubly trained," Sean informed me.

That led to what would've been a good debate, but my next contraction hit, and all else was forgotten. This one was much harder. I checked the machine. The spike was the highest yet. The door opened, and in came my nurse. My excitement doubled as she worked to check the machine and then shooed out Mark and Sloan so she could check how dilated I was. It wouldn't be long until I met our son. I couldn't wait. The grin on Sean's face told me he could hardly wait, either.

Sean: Current Day

I had to get off the bed so the nurse could check Cassidy's cervix. She barely gave me a disapproving look for being in bed with my wife. It wouldn't do her or anyone else any good to reprimand me. Cassidy's comfort meant more to me than their rule. Besides, they'd deliver the baby on a clean pad anyway. I kept my shoes off the bed.

My eagerness to meet my son was growing by the second. We'd been waiting months. He was real to us. The moment we found out Cass was pregnant, he became so, but even more when we found out we were having a boy, and we chose his name. Even Noah knew his name, although when he said it, it came out Nas.

I kissed her hand as her nurse did the exam. When she was done, her nurse smiled as she removed her gloves. "You are at eight centimeters and ninety percent effaced. It shouldn't be long now. Try to rest. You'll be working soon."

As she left, I quickly kissed Cassidy, making sure not to get carried away this time. When I lifted my head, I crowed, "He's almost here, babe! Can you believe it?"

"Yes and no. God, I can't wait. Sean, I can't believe this is our lives."

"Me either. I was thinking about us and how this all came about."

"Me too."

"Remember when I stayed to heal after the car accident in Florida?" I asked.

She got a dreamy look on her face. I had to admit, I loved that memory. It was what ultimately led to us having Noah and Nash. I let myself recall those special memories along with her.

Sean: Four-And-A-Half Years Ago

It had been three weeks since the car accident. I'd been discharged that day and told to rest and follow up with my PCP. Of course, with mine being in Virginia, I had to make do with seeing Dr. Troy in his office because he didn't want me traveling by air, and the thought of riding hours in a car to get back made me cringe. Also, if I stayed, I could spend time with Cassidy. It was a win-win. If only they'd found the guy who hit me, it would've been great. At least the cops had backed off with their attitude. Flanagan had put them in their places and put the chief on notice.

Cass and I hadn't gotten into things yet. She kept insisting I rest and heal. I'd milked it at first, but I was done. I was ready to clear the air with her and get on with our lives. I needed to know what it would take to get her to agree to be mine. I didn't care what it took. I'd do it. The first step was to get rid of all visitors. We hadn't stayed at Everly's house alone. Griffin and Gabe had taken turns being there. When they weren't, other people from Dark Patriots came to visit.

It was a revolving door of company. I knew it was Cassidy's way of putting buffers between us when she kept inviting people to visit. Unbeknownst to her, I'd contacted all of them and informed them there would be no more visits. The next time they saw me would be when we returned to Hampton. No one had objected. Gabe and Griff wished me good luck. They knew what I was about to do without me telling them. In preparation for tonight, I'd ordered dinner to be delivered. I planned for us to eat, then we'd sit down and hash this out. By tomorrow, if it all went well, we'd be an official couple.

I'd anxiously waited for her to get home from work. She'd felt guilty working when I was hurt, but I assured her I was okay to be alone. She didn't do any assignments that took her overnight, although, with so many people here, she could've. I knew she liked her job. It wasn't the Patriots, but I would get her to return once we ironed out everything. She'd left because we wouldn't let her do dangerous assignments. That hadn't changed, but I was willing to talk about the ones I could see her doing. If I was with her, then more dangerous ones might be possible. Besides, it was home. She belonged there. When she returned from work, I sent her to get a bath. I told her I had dinner figured out. She was still in there.

The front door doorbell got me moving. It had to be the delivery person with our dinner. They were early, but that was fine. I'd keep the food warm in the oven until she was ready to eat. Making sure I had the tip in hand, I opened the door. My smile dimmed when I saw it wasn't a delivery person. Standing there looking a combination of upset and determined was a strange man. Maybe he was a neighbor. I hadn't met many of them. Not wanting to be rude, I greeted him.

"Hello, can I help you?"

"You need to leave," he said abruptly.

"Excuse me?"

"You heard me. You need to leave. You're ruining

everything."

"What the hell are you talking about? Who are you?" I snapped.

He stepped closer. I didn't see a weapon in his hands, but I was prepared for anything. I was more than capable of taking him on. He was in shape, but he wasn't in my kind of shape. I doubted he had my skills, either.

"I'm talking about whoever you are staying with her and ruining us. She refuses to go out again with you here. You look fine to me. Go back to wherever you're from, and let us get on with our relationship. As for who I am? I'm her boyfriend."

I almost reared back in shock. Boyfriend! At the hospital, she told me she wasn't dating anyone. Well, other than going out twice. Was this him? Had I heard her wrong? I swore she said there was no spark. Before I could respond to his claim with questions and a claim of my own, Cassidy came strolling out to the main living room, where the front door was.

"Sean, I heard the doorbell. Is that the dinner you ordered? I can't wait. I'm—" Her ramble stopped mid-sentence as she froze.

I partially faced her while keeping the mystery man within my peripheral vision. Her face appeared dumbfounded. She resumed walking and came over to stand beside me.

"Travis, what are you doing here?"

"I came to speak to him. This conversation is between him and I," he told her pompously. I could've told him that was a mistake, but wanting to help him cut his throat more, I added to his statement.

"He came to tell me to leave so you and he could continue your relationship, which I have interrupted.

Something you forget to tell me, babe." I inched up a brow in question. Her astonishment morphed into anger. She whipped her head around to look at him fully.

"You said what!?" she snapped.

"I don't know who he is, but he's overstayed his welcome. Since he showed up, you've completely ignored me. We were dating until he moved in. I know you told people you have someone staying from home, and he was hurt. Well, he looks perfectly fine to me. It's been three weeks. He needs to go. In fact, why don't you get dressed, and we'll go to dinner and talk about us," he told her with a smile.

There was part of me that wanted to go mental on his ass, but another part wanted to see what she would do. That red in her hair was a warning to people if they took it. She might not be a full redhead, but she had the temper of one. I prodded more, but so it would make her madder at him, I hoped.

"Cassidy, I can leave if this is causing you issues. I never wanted that. I misunderstood what you said to me at the hospital."

"Sean, don't even try that. Let me take care of this, and then it's time for us to talk. As for you, let me tell you something. You and—" she stopped.

Walking up hesitantly behind Travis was a guy carrying what I recognized as our dinner. Pushing past the idiot on her doorstep, I handed the delivery guy his tip and thanked him. He didn't say a word, although he did give me a chin lift before he practically ran away. Moving back, I sat the food on the table by the door and returned to stand with her.

"Where was I? Oh yeah, you and I went on two dates. I was stupid to go on the second one, but I thought

I'd give you another chance. I should've stuck to one. There is no us. I told you we could be friends after our second date, but that was it. I can't believe you've been walking around for weeks, delusional that we were just on hold due to Sean being here. My God, are you on drugs? I've got to get HR to test you on Monday." The HR remark told me they worked together, which didn't make me happy, but her tone did.

"I'm not on drugs! And don't lie, you and I had a connection. Why are you denying it just because he's here? Who is he?" Travis demanded to know.

"A connection! I have more of a connection and a spark with my dentist than with you. Hell, that guy who just delivered our food made me tingle more than you. I'm not denying shit. You're rewriting history. I told you I didn't feel anything between us. You agreed we'd be friends, though you've been rather standoffish since. As for who he is, this is Sean, not that it's any of your business. You need to leave, Travis. This conversation is over. He and I have dinner plans, and our food is getting cold."

"Not until you tell me who he is, not just his name!"

I knew she was about to snap, and his tone was grating on me. It was time to end this. I straightened and folded my arms across my chest. I could do that comfortably now. I glared at him, letting him see the killer inside. I brought him out to play when necessary. For now, he was just peeking out as a warning. Travis's eyes widened, and he took a couple of steps back.

"I'm the man she's been in love with for years. I'm the man who loves her and would do anything to protect her and make her happy. I'm the man who won't take you hanging around and causing trouble for her. I suggest you take your fantasy and leave. If I hear you're bothering her at work or anywhere else, you won't need to worry about HR or anyone else."

"Is that a threat?"

"It's a fucking vow. Now, get. My woman and I have shit to talk about and things to do. We don't need witnesses, especially for the naked parts." I couldn't resist throwing the last part in there.

His face flushed red. I tugged her into my arms and kissed her to prove my point. She melted into me and returned it. As I did, I didn't let him out of sight. I smiled when he finally stomped off. I reached out my foot and kicked the door shut, then finished kissing her. When she pulled away, I wanted to protest, but I knew we had stuff to talk about.

"Go to the kitchen. I'll be there in a second."

As she unsteadily walked off, I locked the door and checked the window to see if he was hanging around. I didn't see him. Then I picked up our food and took it to the kitchen. When I arrived, she had glasses out and poured something for us to drink, muttering as she did.

"Crazy asshole. I wonder if he was the one in the backyard that night."

"What night? Backyard?"

"It was about a week before you came. One night, I heard Gus barking. You know he doesn't bark for nothing. You've met him. I went to investigate, and someone was in my backyard, but he jumped the fence and got away before I could get to him. Hank and I talked, and we both thought it was someone casing the place. There had been a few robberies in the surrounding area. However, I forgot all about it after you came. Now I wonder, could it have been Travis? It was right about the time I agreed to go out with him a second time. I knew I wasn't wrong about him, but I did it anyway. I was so desperate to feel something for someone."

I hated to hear that, but I knew I was to blame. I went over and pulled her into my arms. "Cass, I'm sorry. God, the things I put you through. We need to talk about everything—no more waiting. I planned to do it tonight, but this makes it doubly important we don't wait. I'm healed. It's time."

She bit her bottom lip and nodded. "Yes, it is time. Let's eat, though, because I'm starved and can't think if I'm hungry. I promise we'll talk as soon as we're done."

"Works for me."

We enjoyed our food but didn't linger over it. When we were finished eating and the mess was cleared away, we refreshed our drinks and took them to the living room. I got her to sit on the couch with me, as I needed her close for this conversation.

"Where do you want to start?" I asked her.

"I don't know exactly. There's so much I feel we should talk about, but I'm unsure if it all has to be tonight. Where do you want to start? And do you want to go first, or do you want me?"

"Let's start at the beginning. Tell me when you knew you were in love with me. Don't hold back. Tell me how I hurt you. What do you need me to do to make it up to you and help you see that there is nothing I want more than to be with you for the rest of our lives?"

"Wow, you don't ask for much, do you? That's a ton of stuff, Sean."

"I know it is, but we need to get it all out so there's nothing left to fester. Keeping secrets and harboring resentment won't help us in the long run. Go." I waited several minutes as she collected her thoughts. I knew I hit her with a lot. Finally, she started.

"When you came home that first time with Mark when I was eleven, I was thrilled at the thought of having more brothers. However, even then, something about you was different from Gabe and Griffin. Of course, I had no idea what it was. It wasn't until I got older that I knew what it was. I loved them as brothers. I was attracted to you sexually later on as I grew older, and that morphed into love when I was sixteen. I knew I was too young for you, but it didn't matter. Remember that date I went on, and you guys ruined it for me?"

"Yeah, you and Pascal."

"You remember his name!"

"Damn right, I do. Go on." I didn't tell her then but I remembered every man she dated. They were forever burned into my mind. I ensured I knew every time she went out with someone, how long she dated them, and anything else.

"I came home so mad at you, I kept telling myself you would see it and declare your feelings, too. Then, one night, right before Dad died, I went to the office. I knew you were working late and planned to tell you how I felt. I heard you with a woman. It was obvious you were pleasuring her. When she asked about me, you called me a child and said I would only ever be your sister, nothing more."

I felt sick to my stomach. Before I could defend myself, she went on. "I went home and cried on Dad's shoulder that night. He knew I loved you. He said that he thought you loved me or would once I was older but not to hold back from dating and having a life, just in case he was wrong. Anyway, I hoped you were just waiting for me to get older. Only when I did nothing changed. You kept treating me like a sister, and I watched you with woman after woman whenever you were around. And when you weren't, I heard about them. It killed me. I should've given up all hope, but I didn't."

"Baby, about those women, I'm—" but she cut me off before I could finish.

"Don't. Let me get this all out first. I did as Dad said. I did go out with some guys over the years. They were always doomed to fail because I always compared them to you no matter how hard I tried. Those poor guys had no chance. I hated to hurt them. There were a few who I believe loved me or could've if I had been able to let them.

"After Dad died, I went numb, as you know, but I still loved you. I tried to fight harder to do as Dad said. I was trying to fight my hope that you'd change. By the time I recovered as much as I could from losing Dad, we lost Mark."

She paused to take a few deep breaths before continuing. "After his death, when you all took to keeping me out of the missions you thought too dangerous, and I had to leave Dark Patriots and find a job that would use all my skills, I tried even harder to get over you. I'd feel like I was making progress until I saw you, and then I was back to square one. I was excited when you had to take me to help with that mission, which introduced me to Everly and the Warriors. I thought it would open your eyes for sure. Only you kept me at arm's length and showed me you didn't care." There were tears in her eyes that I ached to wipe away. I did with my thumb, but I let her continue. I deserved to feel her pain.

"Falcon was a godsend that trip. He took me aside and asked about the situation between you and me. At first, I didn't want to say, but he insisted. When Falcon found out, he was such a great guy. He said that I had too much going for me to waste my life on a guy who couldn't appreciate me, but if I wanted to try one more time to wake you up, he was game. At first, talking to him was a lark, but as I got to know him, we did become friends. He got a kick out of pushing your buttons. Seeing you with Josie almost killed me. When we got into it, and I told you I was done, and although I hadn't slept with him, I planned to do it. I know I upset you. I felt good that I did. It was a minor hurt compared to what you'd done to me."

I couldn't stop myself. I had to ask. "Did you sleep with him?"

She stared at me hard for a couple of beats before she answered. "No, I didn't sleep with Falcon. During that mission, what kept me going and staying strong other than Everly was thinking of you. When you guys came in to rescue us, I was so relieved, and I thought that the way you held me and fussed over me, you'd confess you loved me when we got home. Except you never did. We went right back to the way it was. I'd talked to Everly about moving away while we were in Dublin Falls. She offered me this house if I wanted. When you acted like nothing changed, I knew it was time to move on and work to get a life.

"That's why I packed my clothes and left without a word to any of you. It had to be a clean break, and I knew the three of you would try to talk me out of it and probably succeed. I got lucky and could stay with my employer and move to their office here. That's where I met Travis. He was friendly and showed me around, so I accepted his date offer. After the first time, I knew we had no spark, but I went out again because I was afraid

I wasn't giving him a fair chance. You see where that got me.

"That brings us to now. I know what you've said, and I need you to know if you don't truly love me as a man loves a woman, don't say you do. I don't need your pity. If by coming here to get me to come home, you thought the only way to do that was to tell me you love me, it isn't. I'll learn to live as your sister. I can't live a lie with you. I sure as hell couldn't live it and find out you're seeing other women on the side because you don't find me attractive, but you're doing it as a way to keep me in Virginia. I'm ready to move on. Being here, I truly think, will allow me to find someone eventually."

I couldn't remain quiet. I moved closer and drew her toward me, although she tried to resist. I held onto her and made her look me in the eyes. "That never crossed my fucking mind. I wouldn't do that, and to hear you even say it, shows me how badly I've fucked up and hurt you. Let me go back to the beginning and explain, and then we'll discuss the future. Okay?" I asked. She gave a short nod.

"Let's start where you did the first time I met you and Adam. I didn't expect to make not only friends but brothers in the Navy. I kept myself closed off from people. I thought it was a fluke when I connected so profoundly with Mark, Gabe, and Griff. Imagine my surprise when I got to know you, Adam, Jessie, and Graden. Coming home that first time with Mark to meet the two of you was amazing. I admit I thought of you as a cute kid, and I was convinced I would come to think of you as a little sister. And I did think of you that way, I believe, over the resulting years. It wasn't until you turned sixteen, when we were home on leave, and you went out with Pascal that I began to question myself.

"You came out dressed to go out, and I was struck for the first time that you weren't a little girl anymore. You were almost a fully grown woman. It shocked me. When you left on your date, I didn't like the idea of you going out. Neither did Gabe, Mark, or Griff, but I sensed it was for brotherly reasons, and I didn't feel so brotherly at that moment. It wasn't hard to get them to follow and watch you. We planned to stay hidden until he took you to that make-out spot, then it was a hell no. You know what happened.

"After that, over the next two years, I watched you change even more, and I kept telling myself to see you as anything but a child, as a sister was wrong. When you turned eighteen, I couldn't fool myself with the child thing, so I stuck to the sister. I argued with myself that if I showed interest in you, it would destroy my friendship and my brotherhood with Mark and lose him, you, Adam, and possibly the others. I couldn't risk it.

"You're right. I went out with and even dated a lot of women. I won't lie and say I never slept with them," she cringed when I said it, but I kept going. "However, from the moment I began to notice you as more than a sister, I did it to forget those feelings you caused in me. I didn't acknowledge it at first. I was good at lying to myself. It wasn't until after Mark died that I fully admitted to myself that was it. They were never going to be a substitute for you."

"Yet, it didn't stop you," she huffed, the pain evident in her voice.

"Yes, it did."

"Bullshit, you went out with plenty of women after he died! I knew about them."

"Yes, I went out with women, but I wasn't sleeping with them. They were all for show."

She jerked away from me and came to her feet. She glared at me. "You want me to believe for the past three years, you haven't slept with a single woman!? Sean, I'm not stupid. You are a very sexual man. I thought we weren't going to lie to each other. You know what, let's stop this right here." She turned her back on me. I came to my feet and rushed over to grab her. She struggled to get away, but I trapped her against me. She refused to look at me, so I raised her chin.

"I'm not lying. I swear it on Mark and Adam. I wouldn't lie about this. I made sure to make it look like I slept with them. The reason I changed women even more often than before was they'd get fed up when I wouldn't sleep with them. I kept up the pretense for you, Griff, Gabe, and everyone else. Even the Warriors thought I'd slept with their bunnies on the rare times I went there. I couldn't bear to touch women that way. I tried to kiss them, and it made me sick, so I stopped. My only release for the past three years has been my hand. And not to be crude, but the only one I think about when I do is you."

Her mouth fell open. I didn't stop myself from kissing her. I need another taste. After a moment of hesitation, she kissed me back. I devoured her. As I did, my erection grew. I knew I needed to finish my explanation, but stopping was hard. I promised myself I'd return to this once I was done talking. Reluctantly, I tore my mouth away. She whimpered in protest.

"Baby, we have to wait. I need to finish first. I hated when you left the Patriots and went to work for someone else. I knew we drove you to it, but the thought of you being in danger was too much for all of us. We couldn't lose you like we lost Mark. And in my case, it was more than brotherly love. It would destroy me if you were killed. But with you gone, I worried twice as much because at least with us, we could put the best with you.

"When we found out we couldn't do the Warriors' thing without you, I almost said we couldn't help them, but Griff said we had to do it, and you were the best choice. Hell, you were even when we thought we had someone from the Patriots to do it. He said we'd be there and could ensure your safety, and we knew the Warriors were no slouches. I kept protesting and trying to make you back out, which was shitty of me. Watching you blossom and become friends with Everly was great. Watching you with Falcon wasn't. I wanted to kill that bastard so many times. Thinking of you sleeping with him enraged me and tore out my heart." I had to stop and take several breaths as the remembered rage consumed me. When I beat it back, with the knowledge they never slept together, I continued.

"When you and Everly got taken, and we had to stand back and let it play out until we could do the rescue, I came the closest I ever have to blowing an operation. I was on the brink of losing my mind. Smoke was the one who kept me from doing it. He was just as worried about Everly, but he assured me the two of you knew what you were doing and you had skills. We had ears in there. Believe me, he and I listened almost constantly.

"Walking into that room where your owner had taken you after the auction and finding him with you pinned to the wall, tearing at your clothes, I lost it. If you hadn't stopped me, I would've beaten him to death rather than let him rot the way he deserves in prison for the rest of his life. I held onto you and didn't want to let you go. I told myself it was time to confess my feelings. I knew you had them for me. Gabe and Griff told me often enough, but after we got home, I wanted to wait until you had time to settle from the mission. It wasn't until I found out you were gone and I had no idea where you went, and no one could find you, did I admit, the time had come to admit it all and not to be afraid of the outcome."

"Why did you chicken out? If you knew I loved you, why?"

"Because the main reason that held me back was still there. It wasn't Mark or Adam. It was the terror of offering myself to you and having you eventually reject me."

"Why would I reject you? Sean, I've loved you since I was sixteen years old! You're not making sense."

"Simply put, I'm not worthy of you or your love. Someone as good and wonderful as you deserve a better man. You know how I grew up. My mom didn't love me. No one after her did until the guys. What were the chances someone like me would get a forever love? Damn, near zero. Sure, the thought of losing Mark, Adam, and the others was a tiny factor, but most of it was that. My whole life, I've excelled at things, attempting to prove I was worthy."

This time, it was her forcing my head down so I would look at her. She was glaring at me. "How dare you undervalue yourself like that? You are a wonderful person and an incredible man. Your mom was an idiot if she didn't love you. And those who came after her who didn't love you were idiots, too. Do you think I give my love out to just anyone?"

"So you still love me even after everything I just said and how I've hurt you for years?"

"I will always love you, Sean."

More talk would have to wait because she pulled my mouth down to hers, and we got lost in kissing each other.

Cassidy: Chapter 8 - Four-And-A-Half Years Ago

Desire flooded my body as Sean and I kissed. Hearing him confess he loved me and finding out he hadn't been with a woman in three years because of it and how he felt about himself made me more eager and determined to show him how much he meant to me. There would be more to talk about, but it could wait. This couldn't. I'd waited long enough to be with him.

As we kissed, I vaguely felt us moving. The next thing I knew, I was straddling his lap on the couch. It gave me leverage to attack his mouth harder, but it did something else. I was able to press my aching pussy down onto him. I moaned into his mouth when I noticed a hard lump that could only be one thing, his cock. Unable to stop myself, I pressed harder and rubbed back and forth over it. He groaned. Then I was whimpering as he thrust up his hips, driving it into me. The sensation of it on my clit made me shudder. I was so primed from just kissing and this that it wouldn't take too much to get me off. He did it a few more times, then thrust me away from him. I tried to fight to get back to his mouth, but he held me there.

Looking at him, I saw he appeared strained, but his eyes were heated. "Why did you stop? I need more," I whined. I couldn't help it.

He groaned. "Baby, if we don't stop, I'm going to take this to the conclusion. Are you ready for that? Because if not, we've got to quit."

"Sean, I've wanted to have you take me since I was sixteen. I have nine years of sexual frustration built up. If you don't take this to the ultimate conclusion soon, I'm going to combust and savage you. We've waited long enough. Don't you think nine years of masturbation is enough for any woman?"

"Nine years of masturbation?" he asked with a frown.

God, here goes. He'd know what a dork I was, and hopefully, it wouldn't make him want to slow down or run. "Yes, I've been getting all my sexual relief from pleasuring myself to images and dreams of you. I want to know what the real thing is like."

His frown changed to shock. "Are you telling me you're a virgin? That you never slept with any of the guys you've dated?" he asked, sounding disbelieving.

"That's exactly what I'm saying. If they weren't you, I didn't want them. I couldn't do it. Does that turn you off? The fact I'm a virgin and have no practical knowledge of what to do?"

I let out a squeal of surprise when he came up off the couch, grabbed me in his arms, and lifted me. He took off walking fast. "I hope you're ready because that there made me extremely happy. I can't believe it. You've made me so goddamn ecstatic, Cass. To know no one but me will have you. Jesus Christ, I hope I can last. Are you sure you're ready?"

As he talked, he got us to the main bedroom I'd been sleeping in. He took me to the bed and stood there holding me, waiting for my answer. Reaching an arm between us, I squeezed his erection and rubbed along it. "Take me. I'm yours."

He let out a loud growling sound, and then I was lowered onto my back. He left me there and stood back. He didn't waste time stripping off his clothes. He didn't have on shoes or socks, but he had on a shirt, jeans, and underwear. When he got to his briefs, I moaned. The lump he had there was impressive as hell. He stopped short of removing them.

"If you dare stop, I'll scream. I need to see you, all of you." I said in a voice that was half warning and half pleading.

He smirked then to tease me; he hooked his thumbs on each side and slowly slid them down until they could drop to the floor. As he stepped out of them, I stared open-mouthed at his cock. I might be a virgin, but I knew what one looked like. I'd seen enough in porn movies and online. Guys seemed to think women wanted dick pics.

None of them, though, were as impressive or beautiful as his, in my opinion. Yes, I thought his cock was gorgeous. The head was domed and slightly wider than the rest, though the width was intimidating. In addition, he was long. My guess was well over seven inches. I couldn't help it. I reached out to encircle him with my hand. That's when I found out that my fingers didn't meet my thumb when I did. I gulped. Suddenly, I wasn't sure I could take him.

He groaned, then squeezed my hand with his and pumped up and down his length once. Taking the hint, I tightened my grip and did it a few times myself. He'd leaked precum, and it helped me to slide my hand as I spread it down his shaft.

"Christ, you have no idea how good your hand feels

or how long I've dreamed of you touching me like this, Cass."

"As long and as much as I've dreamed of doing it. I didn't expect you to feel soft and hard at the same time. I'm a little scared."

"Scared of what?"

"Of how much it'll hurt when we do it. You're big, Sean."

"From what I understand, it'll hurt, but there are things I can do to make it less painful."

"Did it help in the past?" I hated to ask, but I wanted to know.

"Babe, I've steered clear of virgins. I never wanted to be some girl or woman's first lover. A woman never forgets her first, or so I've been told."

"Well, unless you want me to go ask some man to deflower me, you're doing it now." I teased him.

His growl and the way he slipped his cock from my hand made me smile. I yelped when I was pushed flat to the bed, and he was looming over top of me. "Don't fucking even joke about that. You and your virgin pussy are mine. I'm the only one who's going to be inside of you. I'll make sure you can take me. Someone looks way overdressed. I need to even us up."

As I lay there, he lifted the hem of my shirt. After my bath, I'd changed into a T-shirt, shorts, and underwear. I lifted my arms, flexed my back, and then lifted my shoulders so he could work it off. Next, he unsnapped and unzipped my shorts. Tugging them down to my thighs, he ripped them away and flung them to the floor. I was left in my matching bra and panties. He stood there scanning me from head to toe. I got nervous and crossed an arm over my boobs and another over my stomach. Maybe he wouldn't find me attractive naked. The thought popped into my head. I was curling up when he reached out and grabbed my arm over my boobs. He pushed it away as he did the same to the one over my stomach.

"Stay. No covering up. I need time to soak in the foxy goddess in front of me. Fuck, you're so sexy and beautiful, Cassie. I can't take it all in. Or the fact you're all mine. Look at you. I admit that I've fantasized about what you'd look like for years, but I didn't come close. Let me see the rest. Please." He said the last bit as a whisper.

I relaxed and spread my arms out. Taking it as consent, he lifted my upper body. After a few seconds of him fiddling with the hooks in the back, my bra was undone, and he removed it. He moaned as he saw my boobs. I was a decent size. He cupped both in his hands and kneaded them. I whimpered when he ran his thumbs back and forth across my distended nipples.

"I've got to taste these beauties," he muttered a second before he lowered his head and his mouth closed around a nipple.

He sucked and then lashed it with his tongue, causing me to cry out and arch my back to push more into his hot mouth. He sucked, kneaded, and teased for a time before he switched to the other one. I lay there burning hotter by the second. My panties were drenched. Shit, I was close to coming just from his hands and mouth on my boobs.

I thought that was his intention, and I decided to let it happen when he reared up and moved off the bed. His hands gripped the slides of my panties, and he hastily pulled them down and off. I watched as he dropped them, then he went down on his knees. He put his hands between my knees and pressed them open. I gulped but let him do it. As my most private part was exposed, I watched the desire on his face morph and his breathing increase. He licked his lips and then met my gaze.

"You're stunning, baby. I love that you still keep a little bit of hair. Mmm, I've got to taste you," he muttered.

Then his head was between my legs in a blink, and I jumped and gasped as his wet tongue feathered from my clit to my entrance, where he paused to circle it, then back up to my clit. When he reached that distended nub, he sucked on it hard and flicked it back and forth with his tongue. That was all it took. I came. As I flooded his mouth, I cried out. My whole body shook with the intensity of my release. I'd never come that hard before. As I orgasmed, he continued to lap at my folds, hum, and make appreciative sounds.

My face was burning when I stopped coming. Talk about getting off in no time. "I'm sorry," I told him.

His head came up, and he stared up at me. "What are you sorry about?"

"That I came like that. You barely touched me."

He straightened up. "You have nothing to apologize for. You made me feel like a king, knowing our kissing and what I did to your tits was enough to get you that wet and on edge. Your taste on my tongue is amazing. I want more. You're coming for me again before we progress this. I want you wet and ready for me, Cass. I'll hold out as long as possible, but I can't promise how long I can hold back. I want to sink myself deep inside your pussy and make you scream and beg. I need to hear my name come out of your mouth as you come on my cock. I've got to claim my woman. I've waited too long."

"Then get me there. I'm dying, Sean. I need you

to make me yours. Oh, and when it's time, if you don't want to wear a condom, don't. I'm on birth control, and obviously, I'm clean."

"Why the hell are you on birth control?" he barked as he scowled at me.

"Well, I was hoping to find someone eventually I'd be able to have sex with, and I wanted to be doubly protected. Condoms aren't foolproof."

He let out an unhappy grunt, and then he went back between my legs. I guessed I'd upset him with that admission because, this time, he was even more urgent in his licks and sucks. Along with those, he thrust his tongue inside my entrance and fluttered it around, causing me to moan. As he pushed me toward a second orgasm, he added fingers to the mix—first one, and then, as I relaxed, more. By the time I was ready to come again, he had three stretching me and thrusting in and out. He curled them and raked across a spot inside me at the same time as he sucked hard on my clit. I lost it. I screamed this time as I came. I swear, I released more of my lady cum than last time. He lapped it up as eagerly as the previous time. I was boneless and weak by the time I was done coming.

I gave him a weak smile when he stood up. Then I gulped. The time had come to do the deed. I prayed it wouldn't be too painful. I knew I probably wouldn't get off myself. I'd read a lot about a woman's first time, but as long as Sean enjoyed it, that was all I was worried about. I gestured for him to come closer.

"I'm ready. Take me, Sean."

Sean:

I was barely holding back. Finally, seeing Cass naked had been thrilling, but to taste and inhale her unique scent and make her come more than once had driven me to the end of my control. I was dripping with need. The urge to bury my cock in her pussy and pound away until I came was pushing at me, although I knew I couldn't. This was her first time. I had to make it as painless and enjoyable as possible for her. She was more than adequately wet, and I'd stretched her. Hopefully, my preparations were enough.

I was about to ask her if she was ready when she gestured and said, "I'm ready. Take me, Sean."

That did it. I came down over the top of her, and I kissed her. It made me think of her possible reaction to tasting herself for the first time. I went to pull away, but she sank her hands into the back of my hair and held me there. Her mouth eagerly attacked mine. She was nibbling and sucking on my bottom lip. I guess she didn't mind the taste.

As we kissed, I wedged myself between her thighs. Reaching down, I widened them, then gripped the base of my cock and lined it up with her entrance. Her heat scorched the head. I moaned, then pressed slowly inside. Her breath hitched as the head of my cock entered her. I moved away from her tempting mouth and stared into her eyes. I wanted to watch her face as I claimed her. I halted.

"Take a breath."

"I'm okay. It just burns a bit. Keep going."

"If it hurts too much, tell me. We can slow it down." I offered, though I knew it might kill me to do it. She nodded.

I pressed inward more. I worked my cock back and forth until I reached a blockage. I was at the hymen. I stopped. She had flinched when I hit it. "Why are you stopping?" she asked.

"I don't want to hurt you, baby."

"It's going to hurt no matter what. Just get it over with. Going slow is just prolonging the torture. Do it."

Hoping she wouldn't regret this, I slid back a bit. Then I pinched her nipple at the same time I thrust forward, tearing through. She cried out, but she wasn't screaming or trying to push me away. Instead, her legs came around my hips, and she was pulling me deeper. Taking the hint, I kept going until I was buried inside her. I had to stop not only for her to adjust and relax but also for me to savor the feel of her and to keep from going wild.

She was so damn snug around me. I felt like I was wrapped in a silky glove that was wet and hot. I swear she was made perfectly for me. No one had ever fit me like this. I was in heaven and hell at the same time. Her legs eased away, but her hands came down to grip my ass.

"Are you alright?" I asked hoarsely.

"Yes. More," she whispered as she rocked her pelvis.

As her hands dropped, I slowly slid back until the head of my cock was the only thing remaining inside. I glanced down. The combination of her cream and a tinge of blood made me feel like beating my chest. I'd claimed her, and no one would ever see this but me. Looking back at her eyes, I slid forward until I was fully encased again. She moaned. There was the ever-slightest look of discomfort on her face. I paused a moment to give her time to stop me. She didn't, so I did it again. Soon, my thrusts were faster, and I was doing them harder. She went from barely moaning to moaning loudly, and her head was moving from side to side. I saw the pleasure growing there.

Mine was, too. I wanted to ensure she came with me or close to the same time. Snapping my hips, driving deep again, I pressed my thumb on her clit and circled it. She gasped, and her eyes widened. Keeping it up, I teased her clit as I slid in and out of her. I was holding back from going at her full force, but barely.

Suddenly, she stiffened, and her pussy clenched down on me like a goddamn clamp. I groaned and thrust through it, although it was hard to do. As she screamed, my name slipped out of her mouth. That did it. I let go and pounded in and out a few more times, then held myself deep as I came. I growled long and hard as I said her name. We both orgasmed for a long time before we were finished. When I was, I limply sagged on top of her. I had enough brain cells to hold myself from completely squashing her. Her hands were running up and down my back. The kiss she placed over my heart made me smile.

I hated to move, but she had to be sore, and I needed to hold her. Slowly, I withdrew and then laid down next to her. I pulled her into my arms and kissed her. It was a long, sweet kiss. When I broke it, she was smiling tenderly and lovingly at me.

"God, I love you, Cassidy. More every second. How was it?"

"How was it? It was beyond anything I imagined. Didn't you feel me come? And I love you more every moment, too. You know, you did something most men don't."

"What's that?"

"You made it feel so good, despite the painful part, that I had an orgasm. Most women don't get that. I fully expected not to."

I grinned, then pretended to blow on my fingers and rubbed them on my chest. She laughed and then shoved me over since I was hovering over her propped up on my elbow. As I landed on my back, she was up and straddling me. She was smiling down at me.

"Oh, so you think you're all that now. Maybe I should've kept that to myself."

I caressed her face. "No, you shouldn't. I was worried I'd go too fast and hurt you too much. It was all I could do not to attack you like a sex-starved caveman. How sore are you? You should go soak in the tub."

"It's not terrible, but I do feel it. If you come with me, I'll gladly soak. But before we do, I've got to ask. Did you like it?"

I gaped at her in astonishment before answering. "I didn't like it," I said. Her face fell. "I loved it. Christ, didn't you hear how I bellowed or notice how long I came? You rocked my world, Foxy."

"Foxy?"

"Yeah, that's my nickname for you. After all, you're a foxy goddess, remember?"

She giggled and then kissed me. I let myself fall into it and savor the best night of my life. Nothing could stand in our way now.

GSGSGS

It wasn't until the following day that things turned from the wonderful to the not-so-wonderful. Last night, after a long soak in the tub, we'd made love again. It had been even more incredible than the first time. I didn't know how much going without a condom contributed to it, but I had a suspicion it was only a tiny bit due to that.

We were up having breakfast when there was a knock at the door. I went to see who it was. Looking out the window, I saw Hank standing there. Cassidy had introduced me to him and his dog Gus the first week I was here. Smiling, I opened the door. Cassidy came up behind me as I greeted him.

"Morning Hank, where's Gus?" I rarely saw him without his trusty companion.

"Morning, Sean, Cassidy. Gus is at the veterinarian's. I took him in yesterday for a teeth cleaning. He has to stay overnight because they put him out for it. Sorry to disturb you two on a Saturday, but I thought you'd want to know. Someone was messing in the backyard again, Cassidy."

This got both of our attention. "How do you know? Did you see someone?" she asked.

"No. Without Gus, I wasn't alerted like we were last time. You should go in the backyard. You need to see this. I'll meet you back there," he said.

As he walked off, I shut and locked the door. We didn't waste time getting to the slider and then outside. He came around the side of the house and pointed to the back side of it. Moving out further, we turned to face it. As what I was seeing registered, I grew pissed. Cass gasped.

Painted in red spray paint was the word *WHORE* over a window. It was one of the ones in the master bedroom. The bedroom we were in last night. Luckily, the blinds had been closed all night, but still. Immediately, I knew who had to be the culprit.

"I'm gonna kill that motherfucker," I snarled.

"Sean, we don't know for sure it was him," she cautioned.

"Who else would it be? He was here yesterday evening, found out about us, and was delusional from the start. Who else would be here hours later and write that? It had to be him. You even speculated that he was the one the first time. When I get done with him, he won't be able to spray paint or sneak around. It's kind of hard to do when both your arms and legs are broken."

Hank chuckled. "I like you even more. Mind if I ask who, or is it personal?"

"It's some guy at her work. They went out a couple of times. Apparently, he's been living in a fantasy world where he thinks they're in a relationship, and I'm cramping it by staying here. He showed up yesterday evening to tell me to leave. He wanted to know who I was. When we told him and sent him packing, he wasn't happy. He must've come back later when it was dark," I told him.

Cassidy appeared sick-looking as she asked. "Do you think he was outside while we were, you know."

I hoped not, but I thought it might be likely. I lied. "Babe, I highly doubt it. He could've been here anytime between the time he left and sunrise."

"Thanks for lying, but I think he was. The thought makes me sick. Of course, it might not be him. There have been robberies, and the earlier intruder was likely whoever had been doing those."

"No, it's not. Sorry, but I forgot to tell you. My friends at the station told me that the cops had caught whoever was doing those robberies. I hate to agree with Sean, but it would be too much of a coincidence to be anyone else but this guy. It sounds like he's a few bricks shy of a full load. Maybe you should call the cops and report him. I can get one of my buddies to take the report."

"Hank, we don't bother the police with this. I told you that I own a security company. Well, we do a lot more than install alarm systems. We do big-time security and bodyguard work and sometimes do things for other organizations. I was a SEAL, and so were the remaining other two owners. Cassidy's brother was our fourth. If someone is sneaking around, we know how to catch him. Thanks for letting us know. Who knows how long it would've been before we saw this?"

"Hey, no problem. If you need help, let me know. Gus will be home tonight, so he'll be outside on guard duty. Sorry for starting your weekend out with this. I'll let you two get back to your day. Have a great weekend."

"Are you doing anything later?" I asked spur of the moment.

"Other than picking up Gus, I don't have anything planned. Why?"

"Why don't you and Gus come over for dinner? We'll throw some steaks on the grill and have a few drinks. I'm finally all healed up and able to move and drink since I'm not on pain meds anymore."

"Hey, if you're sure, then we'd love it. What time? And can I bring anything?"

I looked at Cassidy. Hopefully, she wasn't upset that I asked him without checking with her. Her smile told me she wasn't. "Six o'clock, and just bring your appetite. Does Gus need something soft to eat due to the cleaning?"

"Nope. He'll be good to go."

"Great, then we'll see you at six," she said.

I shook his hand before he walked back to the side gate. I moved her inside. We had breakfast to finish and a cookout to plan. I knew she'd insist on making dishes, so I planned to help her while getting more surveillance set up and that word covered up on the house. In between, I just might find time for another session in bed. I craved her even more than I ever did.

Cassidy:

I shooed Sean off to let me cook for tonight's unplanned cookout. I needed something to occupy my mind. While I was busy doing that, he talked to various people on the phone. I knew he was seeing what could be done quickly using Everly's existing security features, which, knowing her, I figured would be a lot. He was on the phone for a good while with her and Smoke. I knew he would want proof it was Travis before he made a move, now that he was thinking clearly. He was methodical that way. However, no matter who it was, they wouldn't be happy once he knew who it was.

I still felt icky at the thought someone had been in the backyard, spraying that word, and they could've been doing it while we were having sex. One of the best experiences of my life was slightly tainted by a possible peeping tom. However, thinking about the two sessions of lovemaking and the talking we did before and in between them made me happy enough to push thoughts of whoever it was away. I refused to let anyone or anything ruin one of the best experiences of my life. I'd been waiting nine long years for Sean to declare his love and make me his.

I discovered I had to watch Sean when he wasn't occupied with whatever he was doing because he'd sneak up on me and proceed to kiss and fondle me in an effort to get me naked. I'd given in once, but the next time he did it,

I had to remind him we had guests coming and mouths to feed, including ours. The cute pout he gave me made me laugh. Who would've ever thought a grown man could make such a convincing one?

I was checking again to be sure I hadn't forgotten anything when the doorbell rang. Sean was in Everly's office, so I went to answer it. It was a few minutes before six, so it had to be Hank and Gus. Checking before I opened the door, I saw them standing there. I opened it with a smile. Gus moved inside to bump his head into my leg. I knew what that meant. I rubbed his head. Hank laughed as he shook his head.

"He's real subtle, isn't he? He's an attention hog. He always wants the pats and scratches, especially from the ladies," he joked. I leaned over Gus to give Hank a one-armed hug.

"Come on in, and he's a typical male. What else can you say? I mean, aren't all guys dogs?" I teased.

"Hey, I resent that resemblance," Hank said as he laughed.

"Oh wait, that's giving dogs a bad rep," I jabbed back. In my short time here, Hank had become a friend, and I knew he didn't get easily bent. He moved inside, then shut and locked the door.

"Sean, you'd better get out here and get control of your woman!" he hollered with a grin.

"What trouble is she causing now?" Sean asked as he popped around the corner.

"She's comparing men to dogs. She hurt Gus's feelings."

Gus greeted Sean while all three of us laughed. "Unfortunately, I have to say, she has a point, sometimes. God knows I've been in the doghouse with her more than a few times."

"And you deserved it every time," I reminded him.

"Yes, I have. Hank, I've got the beer outside, and Cass cooked up a storm today. I hope you two brought your appetites. She's a good cook."

Since everything was ready inside, I went out with them. I was happy that the house no longer had an ugly word on it. Sean went and got paint and covered it. He said we'd have someone do a professional paint job later, but for now, it was gone. He got all three of us a beer out of the fridge in the outdoor kitchen. I loved the backyard. I wanted the same thing back in Virginia.

We sat down at the patio set. Gus plopped down under the table. I had a bowl all set for him with water, and later, I had a special treat for him. He sighed happily, and his eyes drooped.

"How did Gus do at the vet?" I asked.

"Same as usual. They love him and want to keep his furry butt. I take him once a year to get a deep cleaning done. It just happened it was last night. I see you painted over the graffiti. Any idea yet if it was the guy you mentioned?"

"No, but I have things set up. He'll be in for a helluva surprise if he comes around again. So, do anything fun today or just relax?" Sean asked.

"Not fun. I got a call from someone frantic asking me to change locks today. She didn't want her boyfriend to use his key to get in. The number of those I do a month is crazy."

"That's right. You've been a locksmith since you retired from the force. I can imagine you stay busy," Sean said.

I sat there and let them chat. It was so good to

relax with a friend and Sean and talk about anything and everything. I popped in and out of the conversation until Sean started heating the grill. When that occurred, I went inside to reheat some items I wanted to serve hot and get the plates and stuff moved outside. Hank floated between us and helped carry whatever was needed. By the time we sat down to eat, I was starved.

While we ate our steak, chicken, and all the other food, Gus happily ate his, along with a chicken breast and his side of veggies. When it came time for dessert, I gave Gus his treat. I'd made these simple frozen doggie treats from plain yogurt, blueberries, and strawberries. They were all good for dogs, but I thought they would be something different. The way he wolfed them down, they were a hit.

"Damn, he inhaled those. You'll have to tell me where you got those," Hank said.

"I made them, and they're simple. I made a ton of them, so when you go home tonight, I have a freezer bag of them for him. It's a cup of plain yogurt, twenty blueberries, and ten sliced strawberries mixed and then frozen. They keep for three months. You can make that batch as big as you want."

"Ahh, you didn't need to do that, but thank you. I think even I can make those," Hank chuckled. He'd told us of his less-than-stellar cooking skills and teased that Gus's food was tastier than his.

It was well past dark when he excused them for the night after he cleaned up. He refused to let us do it. As they left, Sean tugged on my hand and gave me a suggestive look. I knew what that meant, and I couldn't wait. Even if I was sore from the prior times, it wasn't enough to make me say no. I couldn't get enough of him.

Cassidy: Chapter 9 – Current Day

I was there. Ten centimeters dilated and one hundred percent effaced. Dr. Maggio, a midwife, and Zia were all gathered in the room with me as I got ready to push our son into the world. I'd gotten a request from Hadley. She was nervous about childbirth and had never seen someone give birth. She asked if I'd mind her being in there or if I would rather be alone with Sean. I'd had him there for Noah, and I'd been with Sloan when she had Caleb. Sloan had been there when Gemma had Greer. I had no problem with it, so Hadley stood on one side of the bed and Sean on the other. She was anxious, so I teased her to loosen her up.

"Now, you know what this means, don't you, Had?"

"No, what?"

"You're about to see my vajay-jay. I need to know. Does that make me your first lesbian encounter or...," I asked as I leered and winked at her. It took a couple of seconds for what I said to sink in, and then she burst out laughing, and so did Doc and the others. Sean just grinned and shook his head.

When she stopped laughing, she winked at me. "I won't tell, but thanks for letting me see it and watch this whole thing. I won't ask if I'm your first."

Her whole demeanor had relaxed, which was what I wanted. "Honey, I'm happy to answer or show you anything I can. It's scary. I remember when Sean and

I were in here with Noah. We almost drove poor Doc Maggio and his staff batty with that pregnancy. I thought for sure he'd refuse to do it again with me."

"You're far from the worst patient I've ever had. Yes, you had a lot of questions, but you listened and did everything I recommended. You didn't call a million times in the middle of the night for the tiniest thing. However, I'd rather people ask than assume something is wrong. And look what it got me. Repeat business out of you until Sean stops knocking you up and I get more patients. I have her, Sloan, and Gemma. I know I'll get more than a single pregnancy out of them. Keep 'em coming. I might get to retire sooner than I thought," he joked.

"Well, I'm glad you did. You have a way of explaining things that I can understand. Alright, let's get this show on the road. Cass, don't scare me too badly, or you'll have to birth this baby for me," Hadley teased.

"Stand wherever you're the most comfortable. Sean will support one of her legs. You can do the other, or Zia will. As long as you don't block the path to there," he said, pointing to where they had the equipment set up to take Nash.

"I think I'll stand where I get the full visual. Cassidy, I'll hold your other leg if you're okay with that?"

"Go for it, but I think you all should get in place. Here comes another contraction, and it's more intense," I warned them.

Time became a blur as I rode out each contraction. When the contractions hit their peaks, Sean and Hadley would support a leg and hold it bent toward my chest. They helped me lift my chest toward my bent legs, and I'd push. I don't know how many times I pushed and heard he was crowning before I gave a big one and heard the sweet news.

"The head is out. On the next contraction, push as hard as you can," Maggio stated.

I didn't have long to wait. As I bore down as hard as I could, I felt the stretching ease, then a few seconds later, the cry of a baby. I was trying to see him as Zia whisked him away, and the midwife went with her. As they worked on Nash, I anxiously asked Maggio, "Is he okay?"

"As far as I could see, yes. He's got healthy lungs, and he has all his fingers and toes. Let them get him weighed and all that other stuff done. The pediatrician will come in and check him out. Ah, there he is. Now, let's finish this last bit, and then we'll let you hold him and get you cleaned up."

By the time the afterbirth was delivered, they were able to bring Nash to me. His bare skin was placed against mine. I snuggled him and kissed his squished-up face. Sean was doing the same from the other side of him. I felt like crying. Another miracle and a healthy one, according to the pediatrician's rambles. I forgot anyone else was there other than Sean and me. Our little family had expanded again. Staring at Nash, I already knew I wanted another. I wasn't sure if we'd keep going until we got a girl, which Sean wanted, but I thought three was a definite. Hadley had escaped to let us enjoy some alone time. She'd be back when they let the rest of the family inside. Sean gave me a hard kiss. I saw his love radiating from him.

"Foxy, you did another amazing job. Look at him. He's perfect, just like Noah."

"He looks just like Noah did, which means he's

another carbon copy of his daddy. I want another one, Sean."

He chuckled. "Babe, at least wait until we get him on a schedule. Then we can talk. I'm not opposed to another one. You know I want a little girl who looks just like her beautiful mom."

"Well, I don't know if we'll end up with one, but I'll be happy whatever we have."

"Me too. I know you hate to let him go. I do, too, but they need to get him bathed, and you need to be cleaned up. Our family is chomping at the bit to see him, and so is half the company. Let's give Nash to Zia so we can get your brother and the others in here soon. You know how patient he is, not."

He was right. Mark would come soon if we didn't. Reluctantly, I let Zia take Nash and the midwife to help me get situated for company. I couldn't wait for them to bring him back.

Sean:

Our family was gathered around the bed. Everyone was oohing and aahing over Nash. Margie and her husband Chuck volunteered to stay with the kids at our house. That way, everyone else could be here. Big badass Undertaker, aka Mark, kept hogging Nash. This behavior earned him threats from all sides. Gabe and Griff told him they'd slit his throat in his sleep if he didn't give the rest of them their turns. Sloan said they'd have to stand in line to do it because she was about to cut him herself.

He grumbled and bitched, and as each one held Nash, he'd try to hurry them along so it was his turn again. Cassidy was glowing and laughing, watching all their crazy antics. It was incredible to think that I almost never got this. I was so thankful that Cassidy forced the issue nearly five years ago. One of my remaining regrets was the fact I'd held onto my stupid ideas of not being worthy of her or that living with her as her man would lose me the family I gained in the SEALs. Someone should've beat sense into me.

We'd hit some bumps along the way. A big one was when she found out Mark was still alive and that Griff, Gabe, and I had known for four of the five years he was gone. I'd been worried it was too much to ask her to forgive. She hadn't been happy, and I prayed a lot that she'd forgive me. I knew we'd have to confess we knew about it one day, but with Mark being out of the picture for so long, I didn't dwell on it.

Reintegrating him back into our lives and Dark Patriots had been another significant adjustment. The Mark we knew wasn't the one who returned to us. He'd become Undertaker for too long in order to survive, for it not to leave lasting changes in his personality. They weren't changes we couldn't live with. We just had to get used to them. He was a more complicated man than he had been. His time as a biker had made him even more protective of others, especially his family. I was damn happy that not only had he returned to us, but he found Sloan and had started his own family. He deserved it.

When Gabe went undercover to take down the remains of a Mafia family, we had no idea he'd end up meeting someone and bringing her into the fold. Gemma was softer than Sloan but no less strong. She hadn't known him from Adam. In fact, Gemma believed Gabe was a bad guy, yet when she learned the truth, she never doubted him, and she insisted on staying and helping him rather than escaping to safety. She was perfect for him.

Griffin had always been the one I pictured as settling down and having a family. Everyone saw him as the peacemaker, but there was a hidden side to him. He didn't know what hit him when he ended up in the middle of Hadley's situation. It had been barely six months since he met her and her dad. I didn't know what else life had in store for us, but I knew it would likely never be dull.

"He's a handsome devil. Takes after his Uncle Mark," her brother said as he smiled at my son. He'd gotten his hands on him again.

"He is handsome, but it has nothing to do with you.

He got all that from his dad," I informed him.

"Like hell he did. Those are pure O'Rourke genes there. They overpower your puny Walterson ones."

"Oh God, here we go. He said the same thing after he saw Noah for the first time. He loves to pick a fight with my husband," Cassidy moaned.

"It's not fighting. I merely like to state the truth," Mark protested.

"You don't think that chin and his face don't look just like Noah did?" Cassidy asked.

"They do," he admitted.

"Since Noah is the image of Sean, case closed," she swiftly added with a grin.

Mark scowled. "You need glasses, sis. Noah looks like me, and therefore, Nash does. This guy might show up in their toes," he insisted.

As I mock argued with one of my best friends and watched my family makeover our latest addition, my mind flashed back to that trip to Florida and how Cassidy and I ended our time there before I brought Cassidy back home to Virginia. None of us had seen that coming.

Sean: Four-And-A-Half Years ago

It had been a couple of days since the whole spray paint incident. I'd been pleased with the extra security measures I could tap into using Everly's system. She had state-of-the-art stuff. I even found a couple of things I hadn't been aware of. I would be employing them at home. It allowed me to have cameras recording outside at all times with a three-hundred-and-sixty-degree view of the perimeter. If Travis returned, we might get lucky and capture his face on at least one camera. I had no doubts it was him. Cassidy was trying to kid herself into thinking it was a stranger, but she knew it wasn't.

After the weekend we had with Hank and Gus, I hated seeing her return to work on Monday. The main reason was I didn't want her anywhere near Travis. Even if there were people around, I didn't trust him. I knew she might get upset with me, but I wanted him to know she wasn't unprotected, so as soon as she left for work, I placed a call to the owner of the company. After Cassidy moved over to work for them, I'd ensured he knew she was part of the Patriots family. We were colleagues in a way. He worked on different things, so we weren't in direct competition. And it wasn't bragging to say any association with the Dark Patriots benefited him, not us.

All that meant was he was more than amenable

when I called and told him I was in Florida visiting Cassidy and wondered if it would be okay to drop by and see the Jacksonville office. It just so happened he was there for his quarterly visit, which I didn't know. He said he'd love to have me spend the day.

It was around ten o'clock when I strolled into the office. I didn't know what might be required when I came to convince Cassidy to come back to Virginia, so I brought a small bag of clothing. After the accident, I had the guys send me more. Among them was one of my suits. I had the tie, shoes, the whole nine yards. I hadn't known why I asked for one to be sent, but now I knew I'd always intended to do this subconsciously. I hadn't known it would be to scare a coworker who didn't know his place with her. Somehow, I knew business at her office would be necessary.

When I stopped at the front desk, I knew I presented a confident, authoritative image. The woman working there perked up and gave me a huge smile. "You must be Mr. Walterson."

"Hello, yes I am."

"Welcome, I was told to expect you. I'm Nadia. Mr. Trompler is waiting for you in his office. Let me show you where that is. Just follow me," she said sweetly.

As she stood up, I saw her tug on her skirt, and as she led me down the hallway, I swore she swung her hips more than necessary. She wasn't the first woman to do it, but it wouldn't get her anywhere, not now. I finally had Cassidy. No other woman attracted me. They hadn't for ages, although I played the game anyway.

She knocked on an office door, not far from the front desk, and when a man's voice called for her to enter, she swung the door open and pranced inside. When he saw me behind her, he came to his feet. He met me halfway with his hand out and a big smile.

"Welcome, welcome. What a surprise. I couldn't believe it when I got your call this morning. The timing couldn't be better, even if we planned it. Nadia, please get Mr. Walterson something to drink. We have coffee, various sodas if that's your thing, energy drinks, and bottled water."

"Thank you, Mr. Trompler, for allowing me to impose on your day. I appreciate it. As for a drink, coffee with just a touch of creamer would be wonderful if you have it. If not, black is fine."

"Coffee with creamer coming right up. Mr. Trompler, may I get you something?" Nadia asked.

"Coffee. You know how I like it. Thank you, Nadia." She gave him a nod and cast a look at me before she left.

"Have a seat, make yourself comfortable. I have to say, your call surprised me, but in a good way. I've been debating reaching out to you about something. If you don't mind, I'd like to run something by you later." We sat not at his desk but in chairs he had set to the side with a coffee table between us. It was more like a conversation area you'd have in your home.

"Absolutely. I know we don't generally work the same kinds of jobs, but a few times, we've crossed over. I'm usually so busy in Virginia that fitting in things seems impossible. Being here has allowed for it. I've been meaning for a long time to come for a tour here."

"Yes, you said you were here visiting Cassidy. I admit I was taken aback when she requested to transfer here. I never thought she'd leave Virginia."

I knew he was probing, so I gave him something to consider. Cassidy and I had been talking over the weekend. She was going to come back home with me. When she did, she planned to phase out working for them and come back to Patriots full-time. I didn't plan to tell him that, but I could give him enough information to draw the correct conclusions.

"Well, Mr. Trompler—" I was stopped from saying more by a knock on the door, and then it opened, and in breezed Nadia with a tray of all things. I jumped up, took it from her, and sat it on the table.

"Thank you," I told her. My mom hadn't been one to care about manners, but I'd learned them after I met Jessie, Graden, and Adam.

"Thank you, Mr. Walterson. What a gentleman. Is there anything else I can get you?"

"This will do me," I replied.

"That's all. Nadia. Please close the door when you leave and ensure we're not disturbed. Thank you," he told her.

She took her time getting to the door. Once she closed the door, I finished what I was saying as I fixed my coffee. She'd brought creamer and sugar so we could fix it how we liked. "As I was saying, Mr. Trompler, I came to see Cassidy." I paused to take a sip of the coffee. When I did, he hurriedly interjected.

"Please, call me Martin."

"Alright, Martin, and please call me Sean. I came to visit Cassidy. Her move was unexpected, and I came to talk her into coming back home. She and I have been friends for years since she was a kid. Her brother was one of my best friends, which made it awkward when I discovered I had feelings for her. Without going into it, I came here to let her know how I feel."

"And does she reciprocate those feelings?"

"She does. I love her and want her to come home so we can build a life together. I'm telling you this in confidence. What she decides to do about her work is up to her."

He was silent for several moments as he drank his coffee. He was diplomatic when he finally said, "I hate the thought of losing her. She's more than good at her job. She's great. However, I would never want to stand in the way of her or any employee's happiness. I've been happily married for thirty-five years. I know what I'd be like if I was separated from my wife. Mum is the word."

"Thank you."

From there, we chatted while we finished our coffee about trends we saw in the security world. He was fascinated by the Dark Patriots' military background. We talked for almost an hour before he suggested we tour the office. I knew this would likely not be the most comfortable part of my day. Hopefully, Cassidy would hold back her anger until we were at the house. As for seeing Travis, I couldn't wait.

The office was impressive and well laid out. His people seemed busy and had enough space to do their work. Trompler introduced me to most of them as we moved through the office. It took up two floors, so it wasn't until we got to the second one that I saw Cassidy. When she noticed me, her eyes widened and then narrowed. She made her way over to us. I held my breath, waiting to see what she'd say or do.

"This is a surprise. I didn't know you were coming to my work, Sean." Her tone had a slight bite to it.

"I wanted to surprise you. I called Martin this morning and found out he was here, so I asked if I could meet him. He extended an invitation for me to do it back home, but I've never been able to take him up on it." It wasn't a lie. He had asked a few times for me to do it. The main office was near us in Hampton.

"He's right, I have. We've been discussing trends in the industry, and he has been nice enough to appease my curiosity about all things military. I find it thrilling that he and others can use their military training after they get out. I always wonder if our servicemen and women adjust to being back in regular society. I know my son had a hard time after his stint in the Army." He'd shared how his son struggled to settle after his time in the Marines. Luckily, he finally did. Not all service people were so lucky.

"You're right. A lot don't. I know James struggled from what he told me," she offered back. James was his son's name. He worked for his father now.

"He did. Even though he knows firsthand how great you are, I've been singing your praises to Sean. We barely had to train her on anything other than our procedures. She's often our go-to trainer, even though others have been with us longer. Cassidy is very thorough."

"She always has been. It's how her dad, Adam, raised her and Mark, her brother. He was a details man." This got her to smile.

"I'm finishing showing Sean around the office. Are you able to join us? I thought we could go to lunch. I have something I want to talk to him about and would like to hear your opinion on," Trompler told her.

She seemed surprised, but she agreed. Walking through the rest of the floor, I kept her on my right. Martin was on my left. We were almost through, and I hadn't seen Travis. Wasn't he here today? Or had he gone out in the field? I'd have to find another way to drive home my message if he weren't here. Our staff at the corporate office was diving into him and his background. I hadn't made them work on it over the weekend, even though I wanted to.

Imagine my joy when he popped out of the last office. His eyes comically widened when he saw me chatting and laughing with Trompler, and Cassidy was with us. I met his gaze, which quickly morphed into a scowl. His boss wasn't looking at him at that moment. When Martin turned his head toward him, Travis put a smile on his face and came forward to kiss his ass.

"Sir, it's good to see you again. I didn't know you would be here today."

"Ah, Travis, yes, I like to keep my visits unannounced. We're in luck. It coincided with Mr. Walterson being in town. I've been trying to get him to tour one of my offices for ages. He's one of the owners of a firm in Virginia, the Dark Patriots. They do a lot more hands-on security than we do. It's their military background. He and his partners were all Navy SEALs. The tales, I bet you could tell." He chuckled.

"True, although most are classified, I'm afraid. And who are you? What do you do here?" I asked Travis.

"How rude of me. This is Travis Cunard. Travis is one of our threat analysts. He mainly conducts the analysis and passes it on to others to implement," Trompler added.

"So you're not a hands-on, in-the-field guy. Cassidy is great at threat analysis but likes going into the field too much to be stuck behind a desk all the time," I said, with a slight jab of condescension. I knew Trompler wouldn't pick up on it, but Cunard and Cass would.

"That's true. I blame you and the others for letting

me get my hands in so many different things when I was at Patriots," she said.

I could tell Travis didn't like our connection being shoved in his face. When Trompler excused us, I pretended to shake Travis's hand, but instead, I whispered to him, "Stay away from her, us, and our house if you know what's good for you. She's mine."

If looks could kill, I would've fallen to the floor dead. As we walked away, I kept him in my peripheral vision. When I glanced at her, she was doing the same. The rest of the day passed without incident. Over lunch, Trompler asked me about an offer he had gotten from another company to work jointly with them on a project. He hesitated and wanted to know what we knew about the other company and the venture. I gave it to him straight. I hadn't heard the best about them, and if he planned to do a joint venture, I'd pick someone else. Although the work to be done was one I thought worthwhile. Cass agreed with me.

Cassidy went back to work after we returned from lunch. I ended up staying until the end of the day. I knew she was biding her time to bawl me out, but it would hold until we got home. Since we'd driven separately, at the end of the workday, I had to let her go in her car, and I followed her home in the new rental I'd gotten to replace the wrecked one. While I followed her, I felt the hairs on my neck stand up. I scanned my surroundings, but I didn't see anything suspicious. However, I'd learned to listen to my warning systems, and this one told me something was coming. I assumed it had to be Travis, but it might not be. I barely got through the door of the house before she rounded on me and began chewing me out.

"What the hell were you thinking, coming to my

work like that? You had no right to do that, Sean. You should've told me if you wanted to talk to my boss. Why sneak around?"

"Because I knew you'd try and stop me. I didn't expect Trompler to be there. I merely called him to ask if I could tour the office. He has been offering me a chance since you went to work for them. I wanted to see Travis on his ground and make him feel as exposed and vulnerable as he did you by coming here. I'm not stopping until he backs off for good. It won't be enough just to go back to Hampton. What if we do, and he chooses to fixate on another woman? He needs to know that his behavior is unacceptable. He might just be a nuisance, but I'd rather be sure. If you want to be mad at me for the way I did it, then be mad. I'll do anything I think helps keep you safe."

Her angry face softened. I waited. Eventually, she sighed. "You're an asshole, but I guess I get it—just no more surprises. Tell me what you plan to do before you do it. I still work for them and don't want to leave on a bad note once I resign."

"Fine, I'll tell you before I do anything else."

"Did you tell Trompler I was quitting?"

"No, I did not. I did tell him that we're together. If he reads between the lines, he knows it's only a matter of time. He would've guessed anyway from the way I treated you at lunch. I couldn't help but kiss you when you returned to work."

She rolled her eyes, but she smiled. Disaster had been averted, at least for the moment. Now, I wanted to see what my people discovered about Cunard and whether he made any more late-night visits.

❦❦❦

Sitting at the desk in Everly's home office, I stared at the report I had been sent. Griffin and Gabe were on the computer because I wanted to verify that they saw the same thing I was.

"Are you guys reading the same fucking thing I am?" I barked.

I wasn't upset with them. I was stunned and a little freaked at the same time. The information in front of me wasn't what I expected to find when I set the team on the trail of finding out everything they could about Travis Cunard. I thought he might have a girlfriend who complained about him and maybe even got a restraining order against him. Never this.

From what our team found in just a few days, we had a big problem on our hands. It seemed that Cunard had an issue with the ladies he'd dated. Even if they only went out once or twice, the women seemed to end up doing one of two things. In some cases, they up and left their jobs and moved without anyone knowing where they went.

The more alarming ones were those who disappeared. According to what our people found, at least three women supposedly quit their jobs and moved, but no one had heard from them after. Coworkers and acquaintances assumed they had just been forgotten. The women had no immediate family or close friends to report them missing. Our people were top-notch. If they couldn't find them, I could think of only two possible explanations—one, they had help to disappear and likely changed their names, or two, they were no longer among us.

"I see it. Christ, what did she stumble onto down there? We let her out of our sight for a few weeks, and this is what happens," Gabe grumbled.

"Hey, give her a break. It's not like she went looking for a possible serial killer. She needed to get away from asshole so he'd finally get his head out of his ass and man up. It worked. Now, we just have to make sure when they come home, a serial killer isn't left to terrorize Florida. It sounds like we might get to go hunting," Griffin said calmly.

"I say this with all the love in my heart, Griff, but go fuck yourself," I told him.

The shithead laughed, then said, "No thanks. I don't need any help in that department. If you do with Cass, we need to get you some instruction, Fiend."

His remark set off a couple of minutes of insulting debate. I knew it was intended to help defuse our worry and anger about what we might be facing. Once we wound down, we returned to the topic at hand.

"How long do you think we need to give the team to see if they can find one of the missing women? I hate to wait and have Cassidy or any woman exposed to danger. How he acted when he showed up here last week shows that she's a target. He wasn't happy to find out they weren't having a relationship, and I was here to take her. I subtly warned him away from her on Monday."

"Subtle? That's not in your vocabulary, is it? But I guess if you didn't beat his ass, then that's subtle. Look, you're growing up...finally," Gabe quipped.

"Ha, ha, very funny. Come on, Seriously, how long should we give them? Today is Wednesday. Is Friday long enough?" I asked.

They sobered up. "Friday is more than long enough. If they haven't gotten a single lead on those women, then we can safely say there needs to be an all-out investigation. Maybe, if they're available, we ask Everly and Smoke if they have time to help. When did Cassidy plan to move back home?" Griff asked.

"Well, after she got over being mad at me about Monday, I think I have her close to doing it soon. She already talked to Trompler. He's fine with her moving back to the Virginia office. They haven't replaced her there yet. The spot she took was one they had opened for a while, and they had another candidate they were planning to make an offer to when she asked to relocate. She feels bad, but Trompler knows she's coming back temporarily. They'll just continue the search for her replacement. She plans to give them time to fill her spot. I told her I didn't want it to last more than three months, and she agreed. It's way more notice than anyone gives."

"Well, we'll be glad to have her back. I hated her being at another company and, even more, out of state. Okay, we'll get everyone here who can working on this. You talk to her and see if you can get her to leave sooner. Maybe make up a family emergency that came up," Gabe suggested.

"I'll try. You know how stubborn she is. Call me as soon as you guys know something."

"We will. Take care of our girl. Get your asses home ASAP," Gabe added. Griff nodded his head in agreement. We were doing a video conference. As we hung up, I sat back to contemplate how to approach this.

Knowing Cassidy, she'd want to go after Travis and kill him herself if he was guilty. Her tolerance for people who hurt others has decreased since her mission to the Middle East. I knew one thing. As long as we remained here, she would no longer go to work or anywhere else alone. I'd drive her and pick her up. If there were errands to be done, we'd do them together. I'd been doing that mostly, but she insisted on driving herself to and from work.

Hearing the alarm alert to the door opening got me to my feet. I'd lost track of the time. She was home. I'd wait and bring moving and Cunard up after we had dinner. I had a feeling it would lead to a long discussion.

❦❦❦

We were curled up on the couch after dinner. Cassie was relaxed, and I hated to destroy it, but this couldn't wait. I kissed her neck. She hummed. We'll get to that later. God knows we'd need the stress relief.

"Cass, I need to talk to you about something vital."

My tone made her sit up straighter. She gazed at me hard. "What's wrong?"

"We need to talk about Cunard. The team got back to me today with what they have found out so far. It's not good, babe. In fact, it could be awful."

"Tell me. No need to pussyfoot around."

She made me smile. I quickly ran her through what we knew and suspected and had the team doing. When I was done, she was sitting rigid, frowning.

"You have to be kidding me! What is wrong with this world? Is it full of monsters? I swear. You said Griff and Gabe think they can have more definite news by Friday. What are we to do until then? How can I go to work and see him without throat-punching him, taking him out in the swamp, and leaving him for the gators to eat?"

I chuckled and hugged her close. "Have I told you how much I love you in the last hour? You're so damn perfect for me. Honestly, I don't know how you'll resist the urge. I hate the thought of you anywhere near him, even if others are around. We're not leaving the poor women of Florida at his mercy, even if we can't prove he's done something. But I want you and I to consider returning home sooner rather than later. Hear me out. If we do it and he's still a question mark, he'll likely follow us, making it easier to have him disappear. If he stays here, we can always return and take care of the problem. I want to go home. I can protect you better there. I want us to get started on our life there. Buy a house."

"And I want the same. I need to talk to my supervisor. Trompler talked to him before he left, so he knows it's coming. He's not happy, but he can't argue with the CEO. Let me hear what you guys came up with as an excuse for me to leave early. I know you have one," she said dryly. See, she knew us. I told her.

"I could do that. Let me talk to my boss in the morning, and then I'll let you know. I can't believe Travis might be a serial killer, but then again, those men at the auction didn't strike me as deviant assholes, either. You can't judge a book by its cover," she admitted.

"No, you can't. That went better than I thought. If that's all, I have a better idea of what we could be doing right now." I smirked.

"Let me guess. It involves us being naked."

"Yes, it does. Care to join me?"

She jumped to her feet and ran for the bedroom. She called over her shoulder, "What are you waiting for?" I didn't wait to hear more. I got up and chased her.

Cassidy: Chapter 10 - Four-And-A-Half-Years Ago

By the time Sean made it to the bedroom, I had taken off my clothing—not that I was wearing all that much, to begin with. Taking off a tank top and a pair of shorts didn't take long. I'd showered when I got home, put those on, and left off my underwear. It was a waste. When it came bedtime, I had learned Sean liked to sleep in the nude, and he wanted me the same way. I had no problem with it.

He let out a loud growl when he entered and saw I was already naked and waiting for him. I strolled to the bed, laid on my back, and spread myself out. Just in a matter of a few days, I was more comfortable showing my entire body to him. He was always praising it and how much he loved my body and me. The way he'd make love to me told me he wasn't lying. The word insatiable came to mind.

I watched as he quickly got rid of his clothes. He flung them on the floor. I gasped to see he was already almost fully hard. He gripped the base of his cock and stroked it a few times, bringing it to total hardness. I knew what I wanted. As he approached the bed, I positioned myself so my head was hanging off the edge of the bed. I was at the perfect height to reach his cock.

"Baby, come here. I want to suck that gorgeous cock

of yours," I moaned.

Just looking at his muscular and tattooed body and his cock had me getting wet. His lightly tanned skin contrasted with his dark auburn hair, the color of the hair on his head, and that of his goatee. He wasn't freckly like most redheads were. And the tan made his blue-green eyes stand out. I had a few freckles with my strawberry-blond hair, but nothing too crazy, as long as I wore sunscreen.

I knew it wouldn't take much to have me crazy for him. He'd let me give him head once before. I wanted to practice more. My first taste of cum hadn't been awful. I hungered to taste him again, just as he enjoyed tasting me. I swear, he loved going down on me and would keep me coming until he grew too crazy to wait.

He groaned, but he didn't deny me. He walked up to me. The bed placed me with him right above my mouth. I wasn't sure if I wanted to stay on my back and take him or roll onto my stomach. I gave him the choice. "How do you want me to lay?"

"If you stay like that, it allows me to go deeper with how your throat will open up. It's up to you. You're in control. I told you, you never have to do this if you don't want to."

"Sean, how could I resist sucking your cock? I loved the feel of you in my mouth the first time and how you tasted when you let me taste your precum. I'd like you to give me more of a sample this time."

"Yeah? How much of one?" His voice had gotten lower, and he was stroking his cock a tad faster.

"How about a mouthful? You know, you come down my throat like I come in your mouth. I want to see how long it takes me to get you to shoot your load."

He let out a groan. The next thing I knew, he was tapping my mouth with the head of his cock. It was smeared with his precum. I teased him by just sticking out my tongue to lick it off his head. He pushed it more insistently against my lips. When I didn't open my mouth, he sank his hands into my hair and tugged. My pussy got wetter. Slowly, I inched my mouth open. I didn't get it all the way open before he was pushing the head of his cock inside. I stopped resisting and fully opened.

He was a mouthful due to his girth. I had to stretch my mouth as wide as it could go. He inched inside and moaned, but he didn't shove it down my throat. He thrust in and out a couple of times. While he did, I lashed him with my tongue, sucked on the head, and even got to scrap my teeth over him gently. He shuddered and didn't tell me to stop, so I assumed that meant he enjoyed teeth as long as I didn't get carried away.

I reached back and fisted the base so I could pump it while he thrust in and out. One hand did that while the other teased his balls. I did it for I don't know how long until I knew I wanted more. Slipping a hand further around, I grabbed his hip and tugged him closer to me. That caused his cock to slip deeper inside. When it hit the back of my throat, I fought to relax and stop gagging. I wanted him to go further. I'd read about deep-throating a guy. I wanted to be able to do that to him.

"Fuck, Cass, babe, you don't need to choke yourself," he groaned.

I slid off him long enough to say, "I want you as deep as I can take you. Make me choke on your cock, Sean. Please. Do it the way you love it."

"Are you sure? We have time to build up to that."

"No, I want it now. Show me."

His eyes became wild-looking. Then he showed me how he liked it. He pushed to the back of my throat, and when I struggled not to gag, he muttered, "Take a breath."

I did, and then he pushed deeper. He was slipping down into my throat. I held on until I thought I might suffocate. Just as that worry hit me, he eased back, and I could breathe. Several more times like that had us finding a rhythm that let me take him deeper and hold him there longer.

I was so wet I could barely stand it. He was panting, and the flush on his face told me he was close. The next thrust, I sucked him harder and deeper and then kept swallowing as he remained lodged in my throat. He groaned and then warned me.

"I'm gonna come. One more time. Get ready."

On his next slide, I swallowed over and over. He grunted then I had salty cum sliding down my throat. He lightly squeezed my throat, and it lit something inside of me. I screamed, sending vibrations up his cock, making him moan louder. Just as he eased back to let me breathe, he bent over me, buried his face between my legs, and latched onto my pussy. I came instantly. As his cock softened, I could breathe, but I kept it in my mouth as he ate my pussy. He was a hungry animal.

I lost track of how many times he made me come before I noticed his cock hardening in my mouth. I began to suck and tease him again. I pumped the base and teased his balls. It was a matter of a minute before he was back to full hardness.

Suddenly, he lifted off me, and his cock was removed from my mouth. As I tried to go after it, he hooked his hands underneath my arms and tossed me around until I was turned the opposite way, and I was half hanging off the bed. I didn't get my question out before he slid into me from behind. He did it in one hard thrust, burying himself completely inside of my pussy. I let out a tortured scream, but it was one of ecstasy, not pain.

"That's it. Take it all, Cass. Fuck, the way you sucked my cock and took my load, Christ. I love everything we do together, but I truly love the taste and feel of your pussy. Jesus. So goddamn tight and hot. You fit me perfectly. Damn it! I want to go slow, but I can't. Even after already coming. Shit. Hang on," he muttered right before he let loose.

I lost all sense of reality as he fucked me hard and fast. I came two times and was about to beg him to stop before I passed out from the pleasure when he slammed his cock deep, held still, and yelled my name as his hot cum filled me. I thrashed and wailed as I came unexpectedly a third time, milking his seed from him. By the time we were done, I was unable to move. He collapsed next to me on the bed. I vaguely remember him kissing me and telling me he loved me before I fell asleep.

🦋🦋🦋

I jerked awake to the sound of breaking glass. I sat up groggily. Sean was already on his feet. He had his gun in his hand. I scrambled to get to mine as I snapped awake.

"Baby, lock yourself in the bathroom and stay there until I come to get you," he whispered as he slipped on a pair of shorts he'd left by the bed. I tossed on a nightie from the foot of the bed.

"Like hell, I will. I'm your backup. I know the drill. Let's go," I whispered back.

He glared at me, but he knew not to repeat it. Using

the darkness, we eased out of the bedroom door and headed toward the central part of the house. That was where the sound came from. As we got closer, I heard thumping sounds, like someone was running into things. Whoever it was, they weren't a very quiet burglar.

As we entered the living room, I saw a shadow moving off to our left at the same time Sean did. We hunkered down, and then he called out, "Freeze."

Before he got more out, the intruder shot in our direction, but we were low enough that the wild shots went over the top of us. The muzzle blast showed where the burglar was, and we both fired our guns. There was a loud thump and then nothing. It told us we'd hit him. After waiting a few seconds, Sean stood and flipped on the overhead light.

A man in black, from head to toe, lay on the floor in front of the living room windows. Sean went to disarm and check on him, and I provided cover. A loud banging on the front door got our attention.

"Hey, it's Hank. Are you two alright?" he hollered.

"Go answer it," Sean instructed. I did. Hank came through the door with his gun out and a steady hand. When he saw the body on the floor, he relaxed.

"Haven't cleared the house. Stay here with her and him," Sean ordered, then he was gone. While he did that, I went to the body and removed the ski mask. I wasn't too shocked to see Travis's face staring up at me.

"Who the hell is that?" Hank asked.

"That's the guy we told you about," I explained. By then, Sean was back. He scowled when he saw who it was.

"We've got to call this in, although I bet someone already has."

Since I was renting the house, I placed the call.

While I did, Sean called Griffin, Gabe, and our lawyer. Flanagan was going to charge extra for coming to Florida again. Good thing I was headed home soon.

With Travis dead, I was done. I'd had enough of Florida. While we waited for the cops, we went and got dressed. We were decent by the time they arrived, and all three of us were ready to talk to the police. I wasn't worried about our weapons. We had permits for them. Hank, being a prior police officer, was covered, and he knew the guys who showed up.

It took most of the night to clear everything up. We ended up being taken down to the police station. We were questioned but refused to make any statements until Flanagan was there. We had nothing to hide, but it was just the smart thing to do despite them treating us a whole lot better than when Sean had been hit.

By the time we were released, the sun was rising. We were told the DA wouldn't press charges, but they had to wait for official word, which meant we had to stay in Florida. Flanagan was all over it and assured us that by the time the police were done investigating what the Patriots' team had discovered, they'd have bigger things to worry about.

❦❦❦

It was a few days later when everything came out in the news. When the cops went to Travis's house, they found evidence that he had killed those women. He kept souvenirs and a diary detailing how he stalked, killed, and buried them. He was a sick bastard. The news stunned the office, and all anyone wanted to talk about was him. It was a relief when we were told we were free to leave Florida and no charges would be filed against us. I was more than ready to go home.

Another discovery was made in that diary. The truck that ran the red light and hit Sean was found in the last place we thought to see it. It was in Travis's garage. It was an old truck he had that he didn't drive. His diary told how he'd been spying on me, and when he saw Sean leave and I went after him, he decided to eliminate him, even though he didn't know who he was. There were ramblings about how mad he was that he didn't kill Sean and how he was waiting to see if Sean left. Despite the chaos and the questions, we were able to return to Virginia the following week. I wouldn't mind coming back for a visit, but I was more than content to settle back where I spent all my life. Doing it with the love of my life made it beyond perfect.

Cassidy: Three Years-and-Nine-Months Ago

I had paced and tried to remain calm all day. It was almost impossible. By the time we went to the doctor's office for our appointment, I was ready to have a nervous breakdown. It had been four days since I took the first test at home. The one that said I was pregnant. This visit was to confirm with a blood test whether it was true. I kept psyching myself out with thoughts that the four home tests I took were all false positives. If they were, I don't know what I'd do.

The first few months back from Florida were filled with Sean and me moving in together. He suggested I live with him in his apartment until we found a house together. We had my family home, but it just didn't feel right to me to live there. Luckily, we'd found one we both loved relatively fast. Then it was waiting to be able to move in, packing, and all that. I'd also left my job and returned to Dark Patriots in that timeframe.

On top of that, Sean and I had gotten married. We didn't see a reason for a long engagement. We'd waited long enough. We had a small ceremony in the backyard at my family home. I cried as Gabe and Griffin walked me down the makeshift aisle. I hated that Mark wasn't there to do it. The guys understood my tears and didn't take it personally. Those we were closest to at the office and

Griffin's parents and friends attended. We kept it small and simple, the way we both wanted it.

As soon as we got that out of the way, our thoughts turned to starting a family. We knew we were taking on a lot in less than a year, but we weren't your typical couple still learning about each other. We knew what we wanted, and kids were something we desired as soon as possible. I threw away my birth control four months after we returned home. Each month, we waited to see if I'd have a period. The first couple of periods made me cry. Sean kept telling me it would happen. Last month, I thought I was, but I had one, although it was lighter than usual. I figured it was due to not being on birth control and my body still adjusting. When I didn't have one this month, I had to take a test. When I saw that positive, I cried.

I'd found a highly recommended doctor and thought I would like him. Sean was less than convinced. His objection was the fact the doctor was a man. He claimed no one, but he needed to be seeing his wife's pussy. I ignored his muttering.

That was how we found ourselves sitting in an examination room, waiting for Dr. Maggio to see us. His nurse had taken blood and urine. I was chewing on my thumbnail.

Sean took it out of my mouth. "Babe, stop. You're almost to the point of bleeding. If, for some reason, it isn't positive, we'll just go home, get naked, and try over and over. I will get you pregnant, I swear." He gave me a leer as he said it. I giggled at him.

"That sounds like a plan," a man's voice said, causing us to jump. We hadn't heard him knock or open the door. Standing by the door was a middle-aged man, smiling as he held out his hand.

"Hello, sorry about that. I'm Dr. Maggio, and you're Sean and Cassidy Walterson, correct?"

"Yes, that's right," Sean said as he shook his hand, and then I did.

"Whew, thank goodness. Otherwise, it would've been awkward if I had the wrong room and said this to you. Congratulations, you're pregnant. Feel free to go home and have sex if you want, but there's no need to do it other than for fun," Dr. Maggio said with a wink.

We both gaped at him, and then Sean let out a loud whoop, lifted me out of the chair, and swung me around. The tears let loose as I hugged him and absorbed the news. We were going to be parents. I was getting my final dream. Dr. Maggio let us celebrate for a few minutes before he got down to business. By the time we left that appointment, I knew there was no one I wanted taking care of me and our baby than him. Sean agreed.

On the way home, we called Gabe and Griffin and asked them to come for dinner. We'd give them the great news. The only damper on my happiness, which lasted only a few minutes, was that Mark and Dad weren't here to celebrate with us. But I knew they were watching us and were thrilled.

As we pulled into the driveway, and Sean gave me that sexy smirk of his, I knew what we'd be doing until the guys came. I guess we'd be having sex for pleasure, not to knock me up, just as Dr. Maggio had joked. It had been a long and challenging road, but we made it. Sean had redeemed himself in both our eyes, and God willing, there were years and years ahead of us enjoying each other and our family.

The End Until Beau's Retribution
Book 4 of the Dark Patriots